Lisa tilted her face and gazed up at the stars. They were sharp and clear in the desert night.

"It's so beautiful here. I love it," she said softly.

Tuareg leaned over and brushed his lips against hers.

She blinked and stepped back, startled.

He watched her carefully, then gently drew her away from the main path and into the shadows. Enfolding her in his arms, he pulled her close and kissed her again. This was no mere brush of lips, but the powerful kiss of a determined man. After a second's hesitation, she returned the kiss, moving her mouth against his, opening for him when he teased. Heat seemed to spread from the soles of her feet to the top of her head. Breathing became difficult, but not needed.

She had all she'd ever want in life with this kiss.

Dear Reader,

Rescued by the Sheikh is my forty-fifth book with Harlequin. It's the story of two lonely people. One has not had much love in her life. A photographer by trade, Lisa is exploring the world when she signs on for an archaeological dig in the Arabian country of Moquansaid. When she falls for a dashing sheikh, she longs for what cannot be. Tuareg has known and lost love. His childhood sweetheart became his wife, only to tragically die a few years into their marriage. His heart was shattered, and he knows he will never find love again. But when a sudden sandstorm has Lisa rescued by the sheikh, life changes for them both.

Harlequin Romance® stories entertain and touch the heart. I hope this does that for you, Dear Reader!

All the best,

Barbara

BARBARA McMAHON

Rescued by the Sheikh

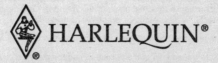

TORONTO • NEW YORK • LONDON
AMSTERDAM • PARIS • SYDNEY • HAMBURG
STOCKHOLM • ATHENS • TOKYO • MILAN • MADRID
PRAGUE • WARSAW • BUDAPEST • AUCKLAND

ISBN-13: 978-0-373-17494-2
ISBN-10:   0-373-17494-2

RESCUED BY THE SHEIKH

First North American Publication 2008.

Printed in U.S.A.

Barbara McMahon was born and raised in the United States South, but settled in California after spending a year flying around the world for an international airline. After settling down to raise a family and work for a computer firm, she began writing when her children started school. Now, feeling fortunate in realizing a long-held dream of quitting her day job and writing full-time, she and her husband have moved to the Sierra Nevada mountains of California, where she finds her desire to write is stronger than ever. With the beauty of the mountains visible from her windows, and the pace of life slower than the hectic San Francisco Bay Area, where they previously resided, she finds more time than ever to think up stories and characters and share them with others through writing. Barbara loves to hear from readers. You can reach her at P.O. Box 977, Pioneer, CA 95666-0977. Readers can also contact Barbara at her Web site, www.barbaramcmahon.com.

Don't miss Barbara's emotionally compelling duet,
UNEXPECTEDLY EXPECTING!
The Pregnancy Promise—June
Parents in Training—July
Only from Harlequin Romance®.

*To Leslie McLaughlin—fellow genealogist
and writer. You are missed, dear friend.*

CHAPTER ONE

LISA SULLINGER stopped the Jeep near the ancient structure and turned off the engine. The silence was complete. Only the ticking of the motor as it cooled could be heard. She had been in Moquansaid six weeks and loved the days she could spend exploring on her own. The desolate countryside spoke to her with whispers of secrets hundreds of years old. The raw umber color gave an ageless feel to a land that was as old as time. The sights she captured on film were unlike any photographs she'd taken in the United States. There was something special about this land and she cherished each moment, each image captured.

Now she gazed at the abandoned dwelling with fascination.

The terra-cotta structure was the only building as far as the eye could see. In the distance, mountains rose to the clear blue sky, their edges softened by restless winds. Several miles behind her was the archeological dig she was working on. Today was her free day and she was once again exploring.

Climbing out of the Jeep, she reached for her camera and bag. Her sturdy shoes protected her feet from the shifting sand. The jeans were hot, but she needed their protection. Her loose-fitting top was the only concession to the heat. Even after being exposed to the climate for weeks, she wasn't used to the constant high temperatures. Seattle had cooler weather—and lots more moisture in the air.

There was little vegetation growing. A few scrubby bushes struggled near the open doorway. Sparse clumps of grass grew in scattered disarray. She looked around, searching for a water source. She'd learned quickly nothing lived in this arid land without a constant water supply. There must be a well or seep or something or no one would have built a house and made a home here.

Outside stairs climbed to the flat roof. There was no glass on any window, the thick walls kept the interior in perpetual shade, and the open spaces gave ventilation. Lisa knew she'd find a dirt floor and little left to define the family who had once worked the land. The wooden door stood ajar. She peeped inside. The interior seemed dark after the dazzling afternoon sun. Gradually, her eyes grew used to the dim light. Drifts of sand filled the corners. There was no furniture. She walked through the three rooms that comprised the dwelling, trying to imagine the family that once lived here. How had they eked out a living? Nomads roamed the land, moving their sheep from place to place to let them graze on the limited grasses that grew. The oasis where the team was excavating was the only place for miles that had abundant water—it even had shade, with palm trees surrounding the site.

She went to each window taking her time to gaze out, wondering what it would have been like to live here a hundred years ago. Life would have been hard. But the beauty of the Arabian desert captured her heart. She had never been in a desert before and found every bit of it fascinating.

Snapping a few pictures, she felt dissatisfied. This didn't really capture the feeling she was searching for. Enchanted with the harsh setting of the land, the contrasts she unexpectedly discovered between barren sand and lush oasis, flat scrub and tall mountains, she wanted to portray this stark beauty with the intent of having another book published. She had enjoyed some small success with two books already. This one had to be extra special. Like the land she was visiting.

Going outside, Lisa climbed the stairs, gingerly testing each step to make sure it would hold her. She didn't want to fall through! Once on the roof, she kept to the edges, knowing they would be the strongest parts of the structure.

Looking around, she smiled her delight. From here the view was spectacular. She waited a moment before raising the camera to her eye. The illusion of coolness given by the mountains had her longing for shade and a cold drink. But she was on a mission—she only had one day each week when she could borrow one of the Jeeps, and they were scheduled to wrap up the dig before fall, so her time was limited.

She relished each opportunity to take photographs of the unusual and the beautiful. Too many people were ignorant about this area. If her photographs could highlight the people and places, it would help foster a bit more understanding between cultures. Plus, it would give untold numbers a chance to view places they'd never be able to visit.

Turning to face the south, she followed the changing landscape from hilly to flat, from scrub-covered to open sand.

She raised her camera and began to snap pictures.

Once satisfied she'd captured this scene to the best of her ability, she leaned against the parapet that surrounded the roof and gazed into the distance, her mind full of imaginative thoughts. She hoped she could do justice to the haunting beauty of this solitary place. Moquansaid had an ancient history. The dig she was working on as photographer was tied to one of the ancient trade routes. Had the caravans marched by this place as well? Had long-ago inhabitants watched, dreaming of the far-off lands they'd never see? She could almost hear the stomp of camels, the calls of their handlers.

Lisa turned one more time, not imagining the soft rumble of thunder she heard in the distance. Was a storm brewing? She scanned the sky, it was still clear and blue. A slight breeze from the west caressed her cheeks. She shivered involuntarily. She hated thunderstorms.

Glancing at her watch, she noted it was time to head back to the dig. Dinner would be served in a few hours and she was thirsty. She had the requisite three bottles of water in the Jeep, but wanted to make sure she never got down to the last one.

Descending the steep stairs was harder than going up. A gust of wind strong enough to knock her against the wall came from nowhere, startling her. She scrambled for a hold, losing her balance and slipping on the step. She fell almost halfway down. The hard edge of the stones bruised her legs and hands. But when she stopped falling, it was the throbbing in her ankle that worried her the most.

Slowly she sat up and checked her camera. A scrape

on the edge, but it looked intact beyond that. She'd hate to lose her camera—or what she had on this roll of film.

Using the wall for leverage, she tried to rise. Instant pain shot up her right leg. She sank down with a groan. The ankle that had been throbbing now burned with agony.

She rubbed it gently, feeling it swell even as she massaged.

Great, how was she to drive back to the camp if she couldn't use her right ankle? The Jeep was old and cranky—and a stick shift to boot. She needed both feet to drive the thing. Maybe it was a temporary knock that would ease if she just rested it for a little while.

The rumbling she'd heard earlier sounded louder. She looked up. The sky overhead remained cloudless despite the increase in the wind. It was blowing steadily now from the southwest. She bit her lip in apprehension. She disliked thunderstorms and certainly didn't want to be caught in one alone. At least being with others helped her maintain some control when the horrific memories threatened.

But with a cloudless sky, could that be thunder? Maybe it was the echo of a jet high in the sky.

She searched to the west, stunned to see what looked like a dark brown cloud sinking to the horizon. Two brief rainstorms had caught them unaware at the dig during the last couple of weeks. The rain poured furiously down for about ten minutes, yet before an hour had elapsed, all traces disappeared. The desert was a thirsty place.

Unless her ankle made a miraculous recovery in the next five seconds, she was going to be caught in the storm. Flashes of that night in the rain she'd lived through as a child danced in her mind.

The thunder sounded continually now. She inched closer to the building, remembering. Could she get inside and out of the rain in time? The roof had seemed solid, it had supported her weight when she'd been on it. If she stayed away from the open windows, she should at least keep dry.

Not like the night that had taken her mother's life. She'd been drenched for hours before rescue workers found them. Lisa inched closer to the house, trying to forget the trauma of her childhood, seeking shelter from the coming rain.

She scooted a bit more. Her hands were scraped and stung from trying to stop her fall. She could hardly rest her injured foot on the ground—it hurt under its own weight. Her camera and case were slung across her shoulder, both her hands were free. Maybe she could crawl. She did not want to get wet. She might not be able to shut out the sound of the storm, but she could avoid a repetition of the night that had changed her life.

The cloud was growing closer. She had to move.

Suddenly a man on a black horse appeared on the horizon. She watched in amazement as he rode the steed at top speed directly toward the building. In only seconds she recognized the traditional Arab robes and headpiece—the trailing end was wrapped across the man's face, leaving only his eyes visible.

The horse scarcely slowed when he reached the house. The man jumped off and caught a glimpse of Lisa.

He spoke in Arabic.

She shook her head, not knowing how to communicate. A glance over his shoulder had her eyes widening in dismay. The brown cloud was closer, blotting out the horizon to the southwest.

"English?" he said.

She looked at him. "Yes. What's that?" She looked back at the bank of clouds. It wasn't a thunderstorm after all. It didn't look like a tornado, but it appeared ominous.

"Come on," he said, motioning her to the doorway, already leading his horse there.

"I can't walk," she said, mesmerized by the clouds. "I've sprained my ankle." The noise was growing, like a freight train.

He muttered something, then came and stooped to pick her up, camera, case and all.

"There's no time," he said, almost running into the building, the horse right at his shoulder. "Sandstorm," he said, flinging a cloth over the horse's head and then wrapping himself and Lisa in his loose robe and sinking down against the wall.

She was nose to nose with a stranger, sitting across his lap, wrapped in the cotton material that smelled like sunshine.

Before she could protest, however, the wind began to howl. Stinging grit hit her arm and hands. She could feel the air pressure change. Her heart pounded. Fear tasted bitter in her mouth. It was different yet like the night she'd waited so long for help. No rain, but the noise was deafening.

"Ow," she said, pulling her hands in against her chest, between herself and the stranger. He wrapped his arms more tightly around her and lowered his head. He tugged the material over them better and leaned against the wall. Despite the thick walls of the house, the air was filled with sand. The cloth sheltered them, cocooned them.

Lisa could hear nothing beyond the rage of the

wind and the sound of sand hitting against the old structure. If she'd been caught outside in this, she wouldn't have survived.

Snuggling closer to her rescuer, she forgot about her ankle, her pictures, even her memories of the automobile accident. She couldn't imagine the havoc this wind would cause. Right now it was hard to breathe. Even wrapped in the cloth, sand seemed to permeate everywhere. She shifted slightly, her nose pressed against his neck. She could smell the male scent of him, mixed with the dry sand. The shrieking wind almost made her deaf. How was the poor horse faring?

Time seemed suspended. All normal senses were gone, only the pounding of her heart, the difficulty breathing and the relentless wind had any meaning. She could feel the strong arms holding her, was grateful for the protection the cotton cloth afforded. She wished the wind would stop. The surreal sound, the constant bombardment of sand was driving her crazy. Would it never cease? She could hardly breathe, couldn't think, could only exist and cling to the stranger.

And remember a dark night on a deserted road, the relentless rain, the cold and the loneliness. At least she was tightly held today. She wasn't alone.

Endless time later the wind began to grow quieter, or was her hearing going? She chanced opening her eyes, but could see nothing except the strong jaw of the man holding her. It was as dark as twilight. Would the sand bury the old house? Would they be lost and not found for a hundred years until another archeological dig chanced upon this place?

A few moments later he stirred and pulled away the cloth.

She gulped a breath of air, still full of the musty scent of sand. Dust danced in the returning sunshine.

"I think the worst is over," he said, looking out the window opening. More sand had drifted into the old structure. The horse stood patiently to one side, head lowered, back to the wall beside the window, the cloth the man had flung over his head still in place.

Lisa still sat in his lap, still burrowed against him. Slowly she sat up, feeling awkward. Looking up, she realized her face was scant inches away from his. Dark brown eyes gazed back. How did she thank a man who had probably saved her life?

She made to move, but the pain in her ankle shot through and she gasped, sitting back down hard on his legs.

"Omph," he said.

"Sorry. My ankle really hurts." She glanced around, searching for something to help her stand. The man gingerly moved her until she sat on the ground and with one smooth motion rose and went to his horse. He eased the cloth from the animal's head and brushed some of the sand off his long neck. The black color had turned dun with the coating of sand.

"Do you have those often?" Lisa asked, watching. It was still hard to breathe. Her nerves were settling now that the worst was over. Her heart still raced, however. What if she'd been alone? She would not have known what to do.

He turned and looked at her and she caught her breath. His dark eyes seemed fathomless. His skin was the color of teak, his features sharp and beautiful. She normally didn't think of men as beautiful, especially one with as much blatant masculinity as this one. But her mind couldn't come up with another word. Her fingers itched to lift the camera and capture him forever on film.

"Not often. But always with little warning. Aside from your ankle, are you all right?" he asked. He came over and stooped down, reaching out to brush his fingers lightly against the swollen skin above her shoe.

"Looks bad," he said.

Even his light touch hurt.

"I hope it's sprained and not broken. Is there any way I could get you to drive me to my camp? I'll never be able to manage on my own." She didn't know if it was appropriate to offer money or not. She didn't want to offend him.

"You're out here alone?" he asked in surprise. His dark eyes were steady as they held hers.

Lisa felt as if she were looking into a deep, dark mysterious pool. What secrets did this man hold? And why did she suddenly wish she could uncover them? Her usually practical nature took flight. She was consumed with curiosity about her rescuer. What stories could he tell of the desert?

"I'm with an archeological excavation just a few miles north of here."

"The Wadi Hirum dig," he said with disgust, glaring at her.

"You know it?" She couldn't ignore his changed attitude. Was there something wrong with the dig?

"I was with my uncle when he signed the paperwork authorizing it. He considered it a valuable piece of un-discovered history." He rose and went to the window, leaning on the sill, his attention no longer on Lisa.

"You don't approve, obviously." she said.

"No. I'm more interested in damming that pass to create a reservoir to help the current inhabitants than in learning about ancestors who are long dead."

"But history's important. It lets us know who we are. And the old caravan trails were lifelines for people who lived here and farther to the south centuries ago." She was not a historian herself, but taking photos of the artifacts the archeologists were discovering and listening to their hypotheses proved to be captivating. Couple that with her own imagination and she could almost see the men and women who had lived here generations ago— families who worked together to make the most of their time on earth. It wasn't even her country and she revered what they were learning. How could this man not?

"What's in the past is gone. I'm more concerned for the present." He returned and knelt on the sandy dirt. Gently lifting her leg, cradling her calf, he began to unlace her shoe.

"Shouldn't I leave it on?" she asked.

"I'll bind it with some material to contain the swelling. It would be best if we could get some ice on it."

"There's not much of that around here. I'll need a ride back to the camp. I can't drive with this," she said, watching his long fingers gently minister to her injury. She peeked at his face again. He was intent on the task at hand, which allowed her to study him for a moment. He had discarded the kaffiyeh and she was surprised to find his dark hair was cut in a western style, short and neatly trimmed. She was more used to the scruffy archeologists at the site who hadn't had a haircut in more than six weeks.

He took the material he'd used for his horse and ripped it into strips to firmly wrap her ankle.

It felt marginally better, though continued to ache.

Finished, he stood and reached over to pick her up.

Lisa flung her arm around his neck, once again so

close she could see the faint lines radiating from the corners of his eyes. How old was he, about thirty? He easily carried her out to the Jeep. She was impressed.

Sand was piled against one side of the open vehicle. The seat was covered and drifts ran up the tires. He set her down, waiting until she was balanced on her good foot. Lisa used the Jeep for support while he opened the driver's cutaway door. The key was still in the ignition. He tried it. The engine whined, but wouldn't start.

Going to the hood, he raised it. A moment later he slammed it shut.

"This car isn't going anywhere for a while," he said. "Sand is clogging everything. You'll need a mechanic to get it running again."

"It's not mine, it belongs to the team. Different people need it during the week," she said. She had to get it back to camp or they wouldn't trust her with it again. And she loved her forays into the desert.

"Then have one of them repair it," he said.

"What am I to do in the meantime? I can't stay here. I have no way to contact them. Can you take me there?" She looked at the horse. It looked large enough to carry both of them.

He looked to the north for a moment, then slowly shook his head.

"Too far. You'll have to come with me. I'm staying much closer."

Lisa stared at him a moment in wary uncertainty. She didn't know him at all. Wait—he'd said he was nephew to the sheikh who had authorized the Wadi Hirum excavation. Was that enough to guarantee her safety?

What choice did she have? Go with him or stay with a disabled Jeep, an injured ankle and three bottles of water. If she didn't show up at the dig by dinnertime, they'd get worried, but no one knew exactly where to look for her. Her independence may have backfired and caused her more trouble than she wanted.

"Go with you where?" she asked cautiously.

"I'm staying not too far from here. Once there, I'll call someone out to repair the Jeep. You won't be doing much walking or driving with that ankle," he said, already moving back toward the horse.

"Can you get word to my teammates so they don't worry about me?"

He nodded, never breaking stride.

In only a moment he led the horse over. Before Lisa could say she hadn't ridden in years, he tossed her up into the ornate saddle. A second later he swung up behind her, reaching around to gather the reins.

Lisa could scarcely breathe. His arms were strong and held her centered in the saddle. When the horse stepped forward, she grabbed one of the man's arms to steady herself. His muscles were hard beneath her fingers. He urged the horse forward and they headed due west.

It didn't take long for Lisa to grow comfortable enough to relax, but not enough she'd let herself lean back against the stranger. At least she didn't feel she would fall off at every step. The jarring gait, however, exacerbated the pain in her ankle. She was starting to feel other bruises as well. She gritted her teeth, hoping she could last until they reached wherever he was staying. She tried to remember the various sites marked on the map the senior archeologist had drawn for her when she explained what she wanted for her pictures. She didn't remember any settlement in this direction.

Before long, Lisa realized why. A couple of palm

trees rose in the distance. Anchored by them was a large tent the same color as the sand. As they came closer, she could see sand piled against one side. Obviously the tent had been well set up to survive the windstorm. There was no community, no house or electricity or phones.

"This is it?" she said dubiously. She had expected a small settlement or at least a home or something.

"I have a radio inside. We will contact someone shortly."

When they reached the tent, he easily slid down from the horse and reached up to lift her from the saddle.

It took a moment for her left leg to support her. She clutched the horse.

"I don't even know your name," she said, feeling decidedly uneasy by everything.

"I'm Tuareg al Shaldor, nephew to Sheikh Mohammad al Shaldor. Welcome to my home." He gave a slight bow.

"Oh, my goodness, that must mean you're a sheikh, too," she said faintly, as the realization sank in.

He inclined his head in acknowledgment as if it were of no consequence.

Lisa couldn't believe she was standing with a real sheikh. Granted, she'd been a member of the party welcomed by the older sheikh when their group had arrived in Moquansaid six weeks ago. But she had not spoken directly with the head of state. Their group had left for the dig the next day and she'd met very few people since who were not associated with the excavation.

She looked at the tent. It in no way resembled the canvas ones she'd seen while camping in the U.S.—or the ones they were using at the excavation. First, this one looked to be the size of the living room of her apartment.

It was tall enough to permit him to walk upright beneath the pitched roof. One side was weighed down with sand around the edge. How had it withstood the ravages of the wind? Glancing around, she noticed sand piled up against the trees. The storm had obviously not vented its full fury here.

"This can't be your home. Don't you live in the capital city?" she asked. Glancing around, the two of them were alone in the expanse. Where did he shop? Where was his food? What about a refrigerator?

"This is home when it suits me." Once again he lifted her as if she weighed little. No easy feat when she was also carrying more than twenty pounds of camera equipment.

If Lisa thought the outside of the tent was different, she was amazed by the interior. Instead of canvas or plastic sheets for flooring, there were actual carpets. Richly hued, they overlapped, completely covering the ground. It was dim without interior lights, but enough ambient light filtered in for her to clearly see the divan with scrolled wooden supports, the plump pillows of gold and purple and crimson offering inviting respite.

Brass and dark wood and rich colors filled her gaze wherever she looked. She yearned to capture every nuance on film. It was truly amazing. No wonder he found the amenities of home here. It was far more lavish than any home she'd ever been in.

"There's no ice, but I think if you elevate the foot, it will help," he said, lowering her onto the divan.

She turned her face, only inches from his. His voice was deep, with the hint of an accent she was not familiar with. His English was flawless. She spoke only a handful of Arabic words. And her pronunciation was probably atrocious. She nodded and said thank you in his language.

He glanced at her in surprise as he released her.

"I am honored you have learned our language."

"Not much. I can ask for water as well," she confessed, feeling foolish she had not made more of an effort to learn.

For a moment she thought she caught a gleam of amusement in his eyes. But he moved to the far end of the tent and swept a cloth off a small shortwave radio. In only moments he was speaking. She couldn't understand a word.

Hoping he was contacting the camp, she eased the camera case from around her neck and put it on the carpet. She raised the camera and looked through the viewfinder. She couldn't take photos of a private dwelling without permission and the light was poor, but what a coup for her book this would be. An authentic Arabian setting—out of The Tales from The Arabian Nights, no less.

Lowering the camera, she leaned back on the cushions, scrunching around a little to get comfortable. Before this mishap she'd considered herself lucky in getting the job at the dig. Granted, most of the photographs she took were for cataloging of artifacts—which didn't give her much leeway for artistic creativity—but she also took shots of the site as they uncovered new dwellings or other foundations. The major portion of her work could be handled sitting down and surely her ankle would heal soon enough that she could continue doing her job.

Tuareg switched off the radio and turned, resting one arm on the narrow table. "Your archeologists will be notified. Someone will be out to repair the Jeep tomorrow. And you can see a physician in the morning. For now, it grows late and the sandstorm was widespread. It would be too dangerous for us to travel to the city now. Rescue operations are underway. We'll stay the night here."

Lisa heard the words, but took a moment to fully comprehend what he'd said. "Stay here?" She glanced around at the single room. Lavishly furnished, sumptuous colors and textures. But no privacy. Where would she sleep? Where would he? "As in spend the night?"

Not that she was in any danger, she thought wryly a moment later. He barely looked at her, barely acknowledged she was present. And he obviously did not approve of the project for which she worked. What was she worried about?

"I assure you, you'll be perfectly safe," he said with a hint of sarcasm.

Lisa flushed. She wasn't the prettiest woman in the world, she knew that. But—

But what? Did she want him to feign undying passion, a lust that couldn't be assuaged by only looking, but needed touch and taste and feeling to settle?

Hardly. She was not the type of woman men became passionate about.

Though, for one moment, she wished she were!

CHAPTER TWO

"I ASSURE YOU I have plenty of provisions. There is un-
limited water from the well. And we will be warm in the
tent when the sun sets. You'll be fine until morning."

She nodded, knowing there was nothing she could do
about the circumstances. Her entire leg ached now. Her
palms stung and there was a growing discomfort on one
hip. Without transportation or an idea of where she was
in relation to the camp, she was truly stuck. Might as
well make the most of it.

"Your furnishings are amazing. How did you get
them out here?"

"Some came on camels," he said.

Lisa immediately envisioned a caravan like the ones
of old—a long line of heavily laden animals trudging
through the sand, stoically plodding to their destination,
their backs covered with bundles and packages.

"The rest came in a truck," he said.

The image burst like a bubble.

"Would it be possible for me to take pictures?" she
asked.

"No," he said unequivocally.

She set the camera down, disappointed. The spectacular nature of the interior would have been such a stunning part of a book about this area.

He watched her for a moment.

"Aren't you going to try to talk me out of my decision?" he asked.

She looked at him in surprise. "Would there be any point?"

"None." He rose and went to a dark wooden chest, its panels carved into intricate designs. Opening the left door, he reached in for a bottle of water. He offered it to her.

"Thank you." She opened it and sipped. She shifted again, trying to find a position that didn't hurt, but the mere pressure of her foot on the divan made it uncomfortable.

"Here, let me see," he said, coming back to the sofa.

He unwrapped the support bandages and the relief was instantaneous.

"I know it should probably be wrapped, but it feels better already," she said.

"It should be iced to slow the swelling, but I don't have any ice. I can draw some water from the well. It's cool. Maybe soaking it in that will help."

He left and in a moment returned with a large bucket almost full with water.

It was cool enough to startle Lisa when she put her foot into it. In only a moment her toes began to feel numb. She thought the water cold enough to help.

"Let it soak for a while. Tomorrow a doctor will examine it." He took a pillow and placed it beneath her leg, elevating it slightly so there was no weight on her foot. The ache began to fade almost immediately.

"I'm sure it's just a sprain," she said again, hoping it was true and that her recovery would be swift.

"And do you have a medical degree?" he asked.

"No, I'm merely hoping if I say it enough it'll be true."

She looked around, seeking inspiration for a new topic of conversation. "What do you do that you can live out here and not in the city?' she asked.

"I'm working on a project," he said. "Damming the Assori Gorge."

"That's not far from where the dig is," she said, recognizing the English name of the location.

"Which is why my project is on hold at the moment. I have had to postpone the next stage of construction to wait until the archeological excavation is completed. I am months behind the original schedule."

"A dam will destroy everything behind it."

"Which is why the excavation was permitted at this time and by an outside group. Haste is needed. We had no qualified individuals who could take on the project at this moment. Once you Americans have provided our cultural ministry with all the information found at the site, the construction will proceed."

"And change the face of the earth there forever. Don't you mind covering up a site of historical significance? What if others from your country wanted to stand where their forebearers stood or wanted to explore this land, which has remained unchanged for thousands of years?"

"What of the nomads who could benefit from a constant source of water? What of the children who wouldn't have to trample hundreds of miles each year and could instead be in school learning, exploring, discovering more than the history of a pass through the mountains that hasn't been used for centuries?" he countered.

Put like that, Lisa could understand the wish for the dam. A steady supply of water would change things—and for the better. But she couldn't help mourn the loss as well.

"Are you hungry?" he asked.

She nodded, surprised to realize it was early evening. She had hoped to be back at the dig by dinnertime.

"I haven't eaten since breakfast," she said.

"And that was probably toast and coffee," he murmured, going back to the chest and pulling out fruits and cheese.

"Actually, I had a big breakfast. I knew it would be a long time until dinner. I did snack midday." But she'd never expected dinner to be in a sumptuous tent on the edge of the desert.

He cut the fruit and sliced the cheese, placing them on china plates. He handed her one plate and a cloth napkin.

"Is there anything to wipe my hands with?"

"Of course." In only a moment she had a wet cloth and a small bowl of water. Once she'd finished, she picked up a slice of mango. The fruit's sweetness was a burst of flavor on her tongue. The juice almost more than she could keep in her mouth. Trying to eat without devouring the food was hard, it was so delicious. A slice of peach was next, then a piece of the cheese, sharp and tangy. The blend of flavors was amazing. She glanced at him. He stared at her as she ate.

"Am I dripping?" she asked, blotting her mouth with the napkin.

Tuareg shook his head and looked away. He'd been impolite. It was unlike him to be so interested in someone that he violated the manners his mother had instilled in him. He should be annoyed. His ride had been interrupted by the sandstorm and the tranquility of his life disturbed by the presence of the woman needing help. He could have left her, sent a message to the archeologists and had them retrieve her. But that had seemed too unkind.

Nura had often teased him about his arrogant ways. He'd never thought about it, only doing whatever he thought was right. Growing up as a relative of the rulers of their country had contributed to a certain amount of expectations for having things his way. He tried to temper that with compassion for others.

The thought of his wife brought the familiar pain to his heart. She'd been dead three years and he still missed her with an agony that wouldn't cease. They'd been soul mates from early childhood. He'd known from the time he was twelve that she would be his wife. She had looked at no other man, he at no other woman.

Though fate had separated them, it was only a matter of time until his own death would reunite them. The long years stretched out empty and lonely. He went through the motions of living, but nothing held any zest. Only his time in the desert brought solace. Now that had been disrupted.

He glanced back at his unwanted guest. There was no question she enjoyed the food he'd given her. He was surprised with the sensuousness with which she savored each bite. Surely she'd had fruit and cheese before. But from the way she was eating, he wasn't sure.

"What is this?" She held up a pinkish slice of fruit.

"Passion fruit," he said.

She studied it for a moment, then slipped it into her mouth, her lips closing over it in such a way that Tuareg felt it almost as a caress. Mesmerized, he watched her close her eyes as she slowly chewed. The expression of delight was impossible to miss. For a startling moment he wondered what else brought that look of sheer pleasure to her face. Making love?

Rising swiftly, he went to see to his horse. He had not made love to anyone but Nura and their last time had been years ago. It seemed like a shocking betrayal to even wonder about such a thing with another woman. Especially one he'd just met and who had no appeal to him. She looked very plain, with her brown hair cut to fall in a simple line. Her wide eyes wore no makeup, and her skin was dusted with a light trail of freckles. She was nothing like his elegant Nura.

The light of his life, Nura had been tall and slender and sophisticated. She had graced the embassies of a dozen countries. They had traveled extensively, always seeking the excitement she craved. London and Paris and Rome had been their homes. They'd visited the Far East and Australia, but she preferred the old grace of Western Europe to all else.

Even Moquansaid, he had to admit.

The horse was covered in sand. Tuareg found the bucket of tools, tipped it to empty the sand, and began to groom the horse. His stableman would have accompanied him on this trip had he asked. But he'd wanted the time alone.

El al Hamalaar stood patiently while he was groomed. The routine soothed and calmed the horse and helped Tuareg gain some equilibrium. He'd get Lisa Sullinger to a doctor in the morning, then transport her back to her dig. Life would resume its pace and the days would march on until he was old and frail.

He studied the sky. All signs of the sandstorm had vanished. He could send for a helicopter now, but it would be dark soon and he didn't feel the injury to her ankle was so great it couldn't wait another few hours.

Turning the horse loose in the small enclosure a little

later, Tuareg looked to the west. No clouds marred the sweep of color. Soon night would fall across the land and the sky would become alive with the light of stars.

The time he liked the best. A time to be shared.

Tuareg turned back to the tent. Perhaps not as unwilling a host as he thought he'd be. His guest knew nothing about him. For one evening he could be merely a man talking with a stranger—her ways would be different from his. Ships passing in the night. For the first time in years, he actually looked forward to the evening. There would be no sad memories tonight.

When he entered the tent, it was dark. He'd forgotten to turn on lights and of course his guest wouldn't know where to look for the lamps.

"Do you go to sleep with the sunset?" the voice came from the divan.

"My apologies. I forgot the lamps." He moved quickly to light the first one. The warm glow of the flame illuminated a small portion of the tent. In less than a minute, he'd lit four more. The colors of the tapestries and carpets warmed with the light.

"I'm tired, but even I do not sleep all the time it's dark," she said. The plate had been placed on the floor, the damp cloth on top. She had withdrawn her foot from the bucket, which enabled her to lay back on the divan. She looked settled among the cushions.

He took her plate and his and quickly washed them in the tub he used for such things. Sitting opposite her on one of the hassocks, he studied her. The lamplight added a sparkle to her eyes, made her skin look soft and satiny. He had felt her against him during the sandstorm, focusing on her safety while the wind whipped around them. For a moment he wished he could touch her skin again, just to see if it was as soft as it looked.

"So you are an archeologist?" he asked.

"No, a photographer. That's how I got to come on the trip. I'm a friend of a director of one of the corporate sponsors for the dig. When the regular photographer got sick, he proposed my name and here I am."

"And what do you photograph, the site itself?"

"That, each layer as it's uncovered and all the artifacts that are recovered. Even broken pottery is numbered, described and photographed. The catalog of the items found will be extensive. The photos will enable people to study each item, even if they never get to see them in real life."

He nodded.

"And I'm learning a great deal. The professor heading the project is an avid scholar of Arabic history. His descriptions paint a beautiful scene of the lives of people hundreds of years ago and the caravans that crisscrossed the land."

"With more romantic overtones than probably existed," Tuareg said.

"Meaning?"

"You make it sound like it was a magical life. It was hard. Men were gone for months at a time. There was no guarantee the caravans would not be set on by robbers or, worse, hit by sandstorms like today's. It was not a glamorous existence."

"It was, for its day. They were the travelers, they saw foreign lands and met different people. There are jobs today where men and women are gone from home for long periods of time. Many dangerous occupations. People still risk their lives to seek the unknown, to find adventure."

"Are you seeking adventure?"

She shrugged. "To a degree. This is very different from my life in the United States."

"Your family doesn't miss you with your being gone so long?"

"I have no family." The animation faded from her face. For a moment she looked resigned. "I have friends, but they are excited for my opportunity. No one misses me."

While Nura was gone, he still had family, from parents and grandparents and siblings to uncles and aunts and cousins galore. What would it be like to have no one connected to him by blood? To truly be alone in the world?

The pain of losing Nura multiplied by a hundredfold.

"I am sorry for your loss," he said formally.

"Thanks, but my mom died when I was six and my dad a couple of years later. It's so long ago I'm used to it."

"Who raised you?"

"I was raised in foster care, and was lucky to only have three different homes. Some kids are moved every couple of years. I even got to stay in the same high school all four years."

"Not adopted?"

She shook her head. "Too old."

"So now you live on your own. No husband or boyfriend?"

"Nope." She glanced at her camera. "I love photography and travel as much as I can to see the world." For a moment she hesitated, then said shyly, "I even had a couple of books published of my photographs."

"Excellent. I shall have to acquire copies so I can tell people I know the author." Family was important to Tuareg, even the accomplishments she shyly acknowledged couldn't make up for the lack of relatives.

She grinned. "I'm sure they'll all be duly impressed."

Tuareg felt an odd nudge in his chest. Her grin was infectious. He felt like smiling in return. Her gaze moved away from him and surveyed the tent.

"I was hoping to take a few photographs of your home. It's so unique. Think how it could enhance my book of Moquansaid."

"You are doing a book of Moquansaid?" he asked.

"That's why I was at the ruins. Professor Sanders told me of the site. He's been helpful in pointing out unique aspects of the countryside. Then, before we head for home later this summer, I want to take some photographs of the buildings in the capital city. The mosaics are quite beautiful. And I loved the fretwork that so defines Arabian architecture. Some of the places I saw as we rode through Soluddai were naturally framed by tall date palms. It's very exotic to someone from Seattle."

"Ah, that is where you live?"

"Yes. It's totally different from the desert. We have oodles of inches of rain each year. Here, there's hardly any."

"Oodles," he murmured. He had an excellent command of English. He'd attended school in England as a child. Yet he was unfamiliar with that word.

She smiled again. "In this case, it means lots and lots."

"I have heard the Pacific Northwest is quite wet. Too bad we couldn't exchange some sunshine for rain and equalize things."

She shifted slightly on the sofa and glanced around again.

"Do you need something?" Tuareg asked.

"Actually I was wondering where the bathroom was."

"For all I like to have the comforts of home here, it

is a tent. The facilities are several yards away and quite primitive." He rose. "I shall take you there. You will have privacy, but you wouldn't be able to get there on your own."

"I could hop," she said, swinging her legs over the edge of the divan. A grimace of pain showed Tuareg her ankle still pained her.

"And each hop would jar your injured ankle." He lifted her from the sofa and headed out.

The velvet darkness of night enveloped them as soon as they left the tent. The canvas sides glowed from the lamplight, casting faint illumination for a few feet into the desert. Beyond was inky blackness.

"Can you even see?" she asked, her arm around his neck.

She didn't weigh much, he thought as he walked in the sand. He knew the way blindfolded. It wasn't far.

"I know where I'm going. Wait a moment and your eyes will become accustomed to the light from the stars."

She looked up at that and sighed. "How perfect. I've noticed how beautiful the night sky is here. At home there's so much ambient light it's hard to see any but the brightest stars. This is wonderful. I've wondered if I could get my camera to capture the beauty."

He reached the small shelter that housed the portable toilet. It was only canvas on three sides, the fourth opened to the south. Taking several steps away to assure her privacy, Tuareg looked up at the sky.

She was right. It was a beautiful sight. He liked to ride in the dark on nights like this. His horse was surefooted and moved like the wind. Nura hadn't liked him going out to the desert. It was not the place for her. She much preferred clubs and elegant restaurants to solitude. He now had more solitude than he could ever wish.

"I'm finished," Lisa called. She hated to be dependent on Tuareg, but he was right. The short hops to the toilet had jarred her ankle and started it throbbing again. She'd never have made it all the way out from the tent.

He appeared out of the darkness and lifted her again. She had never been carried by a man before. It was quite romantic. It reminded her of the old movie *Gone With the Wind* where Rhett sweeps Scarlett up into his arms.

Of course, they'd been lovers. That made a difference. This man was merely moving her from one place to another in a way that kept her ankle from further injury. But for a moment as he strode across the ground, she closed her eyes and let her imagination soar. What if he were carrying her back to the tent for a night of love? What if after he placed her on the divan, he laid down beside her, holding her, caressing her, kissing her?

She popped her eyes open. That was totally out of the question. And she'd be crazy to even daydream about it.

Practicality came to the forefront. This man was a native of this country. She should be learning all she could about Moquansaid for her book. A chance like this wouldn't come again.

Once settled on the divan, she reached for her camera bag and rummaged around for the notebook she carried.

"Would you mind telling me a little about Moquansaid?" she asked. "I'd love some little-known tales to include in my book. If you wouldn't mind."

Tuareg turned the lamps low, then settled on some cushions on the floor near the wooden chest. He lay back. "What kind of stories?"

"Do you know anything about the ruins I was in today? Or about the caravans that traveled through the land centuries ago? Or tell me something about some of the notable buildings in Soluddai," she said, mentioning the capital city.

"The nomads have lived on the land since the beginning of recorded history. Perhaps before. We are a land-locked country, no access to the sea, so travel and commerce were limited to land routes."

Lisa listened attentively as Tuareg spoke. She loved his voice, deep and rich with just the hint of accent. She wished she could place it. Not that it mattered. She lay back, closing her eyes to better focus on the words. He painted a picture of a country little changed through the centuries, of a hardworking, family-oriented society that was little influenced by other countries until recent times. Gradually his voice grew dimmer and Lisa fell asleep.

The whump-whump of a helicopter woke Lisa. She sat up abruptly, dislodging a blanket that had been covering her. Glancing around, it took her a moment to remember where she was and why she was there. She didn't see her host. The sound of the aircraft grew louder. Was it landing right on top of the tent? She debated getting up and going to see, but when she moved to sit up, a sharp pain stabbed.

Slowly, she continued pushing herself up until she was sitting. The notebook she'd planned to use last night lay beside her. She placed it back in the camera case, made sure all her things were there and waited for the next step.

When the motors shut down, the silence seemed to echo. Then she heard men speaking in Arabic. A moment later Tuareg entered the tent. His robes flapped as he quickly covered the distance to the divan.

"Good, you are awake. Our transportation is here."

"Who could sleep? I thought it was landing right on top of me. How did you get a helicopter sent?"

"It is mine. I called for it last night." He leaned over to pick her up. "A quick stop at the restroom and then we head for civilization."

In less than ten minutes, Lisa was strapped into a window seat of the large helicopter. The gleaming white paint on the outside had golden Arabic script on the side. The roomy interior had seats for eight. She'd never flown in a helicopter before. She could see the entire interior. Tuareg sat in the pilot's seat. The man who had flown the aircraft to them sat in the copilot seat. Lisa watched, mesmerized as Tuareg started the engines and soon had them lifting straight up. She looked outside. A man stood beside the horse. Someone who had come to ride the horse back home maybe? Slowly the site grew smaller, the tent blending into the dusty sand until it faded from view. The camp passed behind them as the helicopter turned and headed north.

Lisa drew out her camera and began to snap pictures of the landscape below. She didn't have time to frame each shot or decide on the best way to capture the scenes, she just snapped picture after picture and hoped for a few good ones. This was fantastic. She hadn't thought about aerial shots before, but they could add another dimension to her project.

She wondered if she could arrange a helicopter flyover of the archeological site. That would certainly help preserve it for future generations after it had been beneath the water.

The noise in the helicopter was too loud for conversation. Lisa was just as glad. While she'd like to ask about what she was seeing, she was too busy making sure she got as many photographs as she could. When a roll of film ended, she would quickly insert a new one.

Tuareg glanced back once, then seemed to slow the machine down, dropping elevation slightly. She flashed him a bright smile and went back to snapping pictures.

She felt the change again when he began to slowly circle an estate. Putting the camera aside, Lisa gazed down at a large home, several satellite buildings and a paved driveway leading to a road that curved in front of the buildings some distance away and continued north and south. Other homes and buildings could be seen in the distance as she followed the line of the main road.

They were landing. Was this where her host lived?

A car was waiting at the landing pad and Tuareg gently placed Lisa inside. It took only moments to reach the circular driveway in front of the large villa.

The building was the familiar terra-cotta color of so many of the structures in Moquansaid. The keyhole doors and open windows with tile surrounding them encapsulated the spirit of Arabia she was growing to love. Flowers grew lavishly. The circular driveway enclosed a lush lawn. A lot of water was being spent on this garden, she thought.

No sooner was she inside than a distinguished gentleman rose from a chair in the foyer and hurried to greet Tuareg. They spoke quickly and then Tuareg carried her to a salon and set her on a chair.

"This is Dr. al Biminan, a noted physician from the capital city. He is here to look at your ankle. He speaks no English, so I will serve as translator."

The doctor examined her leg, ankle and foot, asking questions through Tuareg and nodding when she answered as he apparently expected. Soon he began to wrap the ankle in an ice bandage. He continued to talk to Tuareg.

"What's he saying?" Lisa asked when the translations seemed to stop.

"He's going to prescribe pain medication. You are to remain off the ankle for two days and see how it goes. His diagnosis is a sprain, not a fracture."

"Can I get back to the digs?"

"Soon. You will remain here for two days. Logistically it makes more sense. The doctor can then drive back at that time and reexamine you. If you were at the camp, how would he get to see you?"

"I can't stay here," Lisa protested.

"Of course you can," Tuareg said. "This is my private residence and if I invite you to stay as my guest, there is no problem."

CHAPTER THREE

LISA LAY BACK in the large tub, soaking up the bliss of the hot water. She was beginning to feel clean for the first time in two days. She had been assured her staying proved no hardship to Sheikh Tuareg al Shaldor. From the lavish displays of wealth in each room she'd seen, she knew it had to be true. The furnishings in the bedroom she'd been assigned were worth a small fortune. This bathroom was almost as large as her entire apartment. The tub was long and deep, and right now filled with hot water and a contented photographer. She raised her foot and looked at her swollen ankle. She'd removed the bandage to bathe, but would replace it when she was done.

Tuareg had arranged for a maid, Maliq, to stay nearby while she bathed in case she needed anything. But for now, she was alone and relishing every moment. In two days she'd head back to her job: the dry, sandy excavation that was proving more interesting than she'd originally expected. But the showers there were rationed. The camp was shared by so many that she was rarely alone except in her tent. This was utter luxury.

When she finished drying off, she hesitated, hating

to put back on the clothes she'd worn for the last two days, but having nothing else.

A knock sounded on the door.

"Yes?"

"Miss?" The maid opened the door and peeped in. "I have clothing for you," she said, pushing the door open. "I will have your own clothes washed and brought back later, but His Excellency sent these for you to wear until then." She held out a flowery dress in light blue and underwear still in the store wrapping. "Do you need help?"

"I can manage," Lisa said, wondering when the items had been purchased. Did he keep a small stock on hand for people who dropped in unexpectedly?

When she finished dressing and drying her hair, Lisa was tired. She'd been on her feet for several moments now and while she leaned most of her weight on her left foot, she needed to use her right for balance. It ached despite the painkillers.

She hobbled over to the door and opened it. The maid jumped up from a chair and smiled at her. "I have a wheelchair for you," she said, gesturing to her left. "I can push you. His Excellency is expecting to have an early lunch for you."

"Your English is good. Is it taught in schools here?" Lisa asked as she sank gratefully into the chair. As soon as she was settled, the maid began pushing her toward the door.

"Yes. I studied it in school. I traveled with His Excellency and his wife when they visited other countries. I liked that. My mother told me I would have better job opportunities if I could speak another language. I also speak French," Maliq said as they continued down the long hallway.

"I speak only English and a few words of Arabic," Lisa confessed, saying thank you to the young woman in her language.

"I can teach you more if you like," Maliq said.

"I would like, while I'm here." Lisa was intrigued with the idea. It would give her something to do. If she couldn't be exploring and taking pictures, what else could she do?

So Tuareg had a wife. Of course a man his age would be married. And Lisa suspected his wife would be as beautiful as he was handsome. Did they have children? For a moment she wished she had a special someone waiting for her as Tuareg had asked about. She had not met anyone to fall in love with. Would she ever? Or was wanderlust to be her companion through the years? Capturing sights and scenes and people through her lens and forever remaining on the outside watching, wishing.

When the maid pushed her onto a large patio, Lisa was enchanted all over again. The flagstone terrace was covered by a high trellis around which vines were entwined. The partial shade made it possible to be comfortable outside in the heat of the day. There was a fountain splashing merrily and a faint breeze. Flowers grew at the edges of the patio, bright red and sunny yellow, contrasting with their deep green leaves.

A round table was near the fountain, set for a meal.

She almost didn't recognize the man who rose when she came out. Tuareg had also cleaned up and was now dressed in casual western attire—khaki slacks and a polo shirt. The knit shirt delineated his muscular body. He was tall and physically fit. No wonder he could hoist her around so easily. She glanced around, but didn't see his wife. Was she away?

"Thank you, Maliq," he said to the young maid. "Your services won't be required again until later."

She nodded her head and quietly slipped away.

"I know you must be hungry," he said, pushing the chair up to the table. He locked it in place and took a seat opposite.

"I am. But it was wonderful to have a bath. Thank you for the clothes."

"They fit?"

"Perfectly."

"Then I am glad they were available."

A servant brought out a large tray with two plates and two glasses with ice. He placed the dishes before each of them and poured tea into the glasses.

A second servant brought out a tray with sandwiches and fruit salad.

"I remember Americans like iced tea when the weather is hot, is that not correct?" Tuareg said.

"I sure do. Thank you. This looks delicious." A flaky croissant was filled with what looked like chicken salad. There was fresh fruit and some sweet bread as well. "Will your wife be joining us?"

Tuareg looked at her for a moment, then shook his head. "Nura is dead. I am a widower."

"I'm sorry, I didn't know. The maid said she traveled with you and your wife, I thought—" It was obvious she thought the woman was alive.

"One adjusts," he replied, beginning to eat.

Lisa also began to eat, wishing she could think of something to take the look of bleakness away from her host's face.

She wasn't good with family situations. Living in foster care for most of her life had left her constantly on the outside looking in. She could empathize with others, but couldn't quite make the connection. Maybe it was why she was such a good photographer: she knew what to look for, she had been searching for special places all her life.

The meal was delicious. The chicken salad was light yet filling, made with celery and apple and walnuts. Fresh melons cut in small pieces complemented the salad. The drink was some kind of sweet tea, not quite like home, but delicious and refreshing.

Conversation lagged as they each seemed lost in thought. She risked another glance in his direction and was surprised to find him watching her.

A servant came out of the house and spoke quietly to Tuareg. He frowned, then rose, placing his napkin on the table.

"Excuse me a moment, it seems I have an unexpected guest." He walked around the table and followed the servant inside.

It seemed to be his day for unexpected guests. Lisa let out a small sigh. She felt awkward after mentioning his wife. She wished the maid had made it clear why all travel had been in the past. But even if she'd known, she'd be at a loss for words. What did a photographer have in common with a sheikh?

Lisa had almost finished eating when Tuareg and an older woman came out onto the patio.

"Mother, may I present Lisa Sullinger. Lisa, my mother, Yasmin al Shaldor."

Tuareg seated the older woman at the table. A servant hurried out and spoke in Arabic. His mother turned and shook her head, then turned back to Lisa.

"I did not expect to find Tuareg with company," she

said, her eyes studying Lisa. "I thought he was still in the desert, but I heard the helicopter earlier and took a chance he'd returned home."

"He very kindly rescued me when I hurt myself at a ruin," Lisa explained. Surely Tuareg had already done so.

"Indeed," Yasmin murmured, glancing at her son and back at Lisa. "How did that happen?"

Lisa explained while Tuareg sat back at his place, leaning back in the chair and watching the conversation without participating.

The servant returned with another glass and napkin. He poured tea into it for Tuareg's mother, then with a bow quickly left.

She smiled at Lisa. "You are eating earlier than I usually eat. I'm meeting a friend for lunch in a little while."

"We were in the desert this morning. This is our first meal," Tuareg explained.

"Since you have returned earlier than planned, perhaps you can now give thought to attending the party your uncle is giving for your cousin's birthday. Your guest would be invited as well," his mother said.

"Thank you," Lisa said quickly, noting the frown on Tuareg's face. "But I have to return to the dig."

"Dig?"

"She's with the archeologists at the Wadi Hirum," he said. "She'll be returning in a couple of days. The doctor who examined her ankle said to give it total rest for at least two days."

"I wouldn't intrude at a family party." Lisa knew better than to be the only outsider at a family gathering. Especially one in which the normal language was foreign to her.

He shrugged. "I'm sure my cousin would be delighted to have you attend. She likes large gatherings and the more interesting people there, the more she likes it. I was not planning to attend." He glanced at his mother and then looked back to Lisa. "If you would like to go, however, I would escort you. Perhaps you could take more pictures for your project."

Lisa smiled, wondering when the party was and how long she could stay away from the dig.

"Pictures for a project?" his mother asked.

Lisa explained.

"So if you do that when your time is free, do tell me how the investigation into the lives of those who lived at Wadi Hirum is progressing. Have any startling discoveries been made?" she asked Lisa.

"Not that I've heard. Though I'm not an archeologist, I'm fascinated by the artifacts they are uncovering—bowls, bits of glass and metal items. There have been a couple of pieces of art, statues that are small but beautifully carved from stone. And all of which are estimated to be several hundred years old."

Yasmin looked at her son. "And have you seen these artifacts?"

"No. I have not visited the excavation."

"Yet you are most anxious for them to finish so you can proceed with your project."

"Damming the river nearby," Lisa said with a frown. She knew, as did all on the dig, the terms of the permit. But none of them liked it. She wished there was something to be done to keep the land as it was. Or at least delay the flooding until all the secrets of Wadi Hirum had been discovered.

"You've heard of that?" Yasmin asked, clearly surprised.

"According to Professor Sanders, the only reason we are there is to rush through finding whatever we can before the deadline. Then the area will be flooded and lost forever. I hope we are able to get all the information of the earlier settlement before it's too late. The archeologists can't rush things too much for fear of destroying an important clue to the past. It seems a shame to stop on a certain date without completely exploring the entire area."

She looked at Tuareg, emboldened to ask. "It occurred to me as we were flying here that perhaps an aerial view would also be of value. Can I be taken back via your helicopter and given a chance to take some photos from the air?"

Tuareg nodded. "I'd be happy to also fly along the river so you can see what will happen when the pass is dammed. And how wide an area will benefit from the reservoir. Perhaps you'll change your mind about the project."

"Are you not in favor of the dam?" Yasmin asked.

"It seems a shame to eradicate all traces of the past," Lisa said.

"But the benefit to the present is what's important. The past should not be more important than the present," Tuareg's mother said, her eyes sad, her gaze on her son.

Lisa felt some unspoken communication was being exchanged between the two of them. Tuareg held his mother's gaze for a long moment, then looked at Lisa.

She felt herself grow warm with his regard. Taking a sip of the sweetened tea, she tried to keep her hand from shaking. She was affected by the man's nearness. Was she going to fall for the handsome sheikh just because he was the most exciting man she'd ever met?

Nonsense. She had more sense than that.

But she thought she might be tempted from the sheer masculine appeal the man had. She wished her friends could meet him.

The sooner she returned to work, the better. She should not be thinking such thoughts. Her place was at the excavation, not at an elegant villa belonging to a fabulously wealthy man. Talk about being out of her depths.

"Have you seen much of Moquansaid?" Yasmin asked.

"Only driving through from the capital on our way to the site when we arrived. Soluddai is a beautiful city. Then, of course, the countryside is amazing. How quickly it changes from the greenery in the city parks to the barren desert."

"We are a small country yet have moved into the twenty-first century with all speed," Yasmin said proudly. Her couturier clothes spoke of strong ties to Western Europe. Did she do her shopping in Paris?

Lisa wondered what it would be like to fly to Paris on a shopping spree. Fabulous, she bet.

"The avenues I saw in the capital city were lovely. I'm especially intrigued by the architecture of the buildings, the blend of modern high-rise glass and steel with ancient buildings of Arabic design. The melding of two different styles is fascinating."

"Lisa obviously has an artist's eye," Tuareg said. "She plans to write a book on what she finds in Moquansaid. Perhaps she can visit the city while she convalesces," Tuareg said easily.

"A book?" Yasmin said, looking at Lisa with new interest. "What kind of book?"

"A photographic one, mostly pictures with captions."

"She's published two such already. I've ordered them. You can see them when they arrive," Tuareg said.

"You've ordered copies?" Lisa was clearly surprised.

He nodded slowly. "I'm interested in seeing your work."

"Why?"

"Perhaps to grant you that request you made at the tent."

She blinked. He might let her photograph the interior of the tent? Would he also let her take pictures of this house? It was beautiful, inside and out. She wouldn't infringe on his hospitality, but she would be guaranteed publication if she could show aspects of Moquansaid that no one else had shown before.

Whoa, she was getting ahead of herself. He might not like what she'd done on the earlier books. He hadn't said yes yet.

"An interesting profession for a woman, a photographer. Do you take pictures of social events?" Yasmin asked.

Lisa shook her head. "I like capturing scenes that will have people thinking or remembering. One of my books was comprised of scenes of childhood. I traveled around the western United States taking pictures of carnivals and county fairs, swimming holes and tree houses, parks and playgrounds. Things from childhood to bring back fond memories for those who experienced them, or evoke a feeling of nostalgia for those who hadn't but feel that might have been a good part of childhood."

"Tree houses?" Yasmin asked.

Lisa nodded. "Perhaps not common over here?"

Yasmin looked at her son with puzzlement.

"A small platform usually in the lower branches of a sturdy tree where children play."

"How dangerous."

"No more so than other activities of childhood. What was the other book about?" he asked.

"Waterfalls."

"That's all?"

Lisa nodded, smiling. "It took me more than a year to get a collection of pictures of various falls. I tried for unusual vantage points. The top of Yosemite Falls, behind the water at Arabesque Falls, at sunset at Niagara Falls with the glow of the colors turning the water into a shimmering silk of reflections. Some are located in the midst of lush vegetation, others ephemerals in an otherwise barren landscape."

"So you travel extensively?" Yasmin asked. "As did my son."

Lisa looked at Tuareg. "But you no longer travel?"

"It was Nura's wish to travel. She enjoyed seeing new places, meeting new people."

Yasmin looked concerned as she watched her son speak. "You could go to those places again," she said gently.

"No." He pushed back his chair and rose. "If you will excuse me, I have some business to attend to."

"I'll stay and talk to Lisa until it's time to leave for my luncheon," Yasmin said.

Once Tuareg had left the patio, the servants quickly came and cleared the table, leaving only fresh tea and glasses for the women.

Yasmin checked her watch and then smiled at Lisa. "I can stay a little longer. Tell me how you came to be a part of the archeology team."

Lisa began telling her about the unexpected treat of traveling with the group. She made brief mention of each member and how they all worked together as a team. Her role was small, yet she felt it important. The topic moved on to the ruins she'd been photographing. Then to the sandstorm and the havoc a bad storm could cause. Fortunately they were not frequent, Yasmin said.

Before she left, Yasmin reissued the invitation to the birthday celebration for Tuareg's cousin. Lisa made a noncommittal answer and bid the woman goodbye. She'd enjoyed talking with her.

The quiet once Yasmin left was soothing. Lisa maneuvered her wheelchair around until she was looking over the garden. Tall shrubs gave a green backdrop for the blossoms that displayed every hue she could think of. The flowers were beautiful. She wished she'd brought her camera.

A short time later Maliq came to the door.

"Would you like to come inside? Rest? Or can I bring you something here?"

"Thank you. I think I would like to go lie down for a while." The next time she left her bedroom, she'd be sure to carry her camera.

To her surprise, Lisa slept more than an hour. She awoke refreshed and was soon chafing at the inactivity. She was used to doing, not sitting. She hopped over to the window and gazed out on the pretty setting. She'd love to walk around the estate. Testing her ankle gingerly, she quickly learned it had not miraculously healed while she rested.

Maliq entered a couple of moments later, several swimsuits over one arm.

"His Excellency wonders if you'd like to go swimming? He is taking a break and offered to take you with him." The awe in her voice let Lisa know the maid was impressed he would make such a request.

It sounded like heaven. The house was cool, but she'd love to immerse herself in a pool and enjoy the unexpected luxury. The excavation site was very dry and dusty. They'd all have loved a pool there.

In less than ten minutes the maid was pushing her into the foyer of the home, where Tuareg waited. Lisa had chosen a modest one-piece suit and wore a terry covering over it.

Tuareg had changed into shorts and a T-shirt. His long legs were tanned and the short sleeves of his shirt displayed his muscular arms to advantage.

"Thank you for inviting me. I love swimming, though I'm not sure how much I can do with this ankle, but I can at least enjoy the water," she said, trying to ignore the small thrill seeing him brought. He was her reluctant host, nothing more.

He spoke to Maliq in Arabic and took the handles of the wheelchair, pushing Lisa outside. He lifted her, chair and all, down the three shallow steps, then headed to the far side of the house. The walkway was comprised of fine gravel, not easy to push the chair on, but he seemed to have no difficulty.

"Did you finish your work?" she asked politely.

"Yes."

Rounding a bend, the path widened and changed to flagstone. The same stones that flanked the pool. It was an infinity edge pool, the far edge seeming to have no boundary, the water skimming over. Beyond was a distant view of the mountains.

There was a hot tub at one end. The main pool was Olympic size, with lanes clearly delineated.

"Wow," she said softly. Several tall palms shaded a portion of the flagstone. The coping, along with the pool itself, was in the full afternoon sunshine.

"You do swim?" he said, stopping the chair near the edge.

"Yes." Suddenly she felt shy about taking off her cover-up.

Tuareg had no such qualms. He quickly pulled his shirt off and soon kicked off his shorts.

Lisa stared. He was gorgeous. His shoulders were wide and bronzed. His muscles were sculptural. He glanced at her, raising an eyebrow.

She looked away and hoped the heat that rose in her face wasn't turning her skin as red as it felt. She took off the cover-up and, using the arms of the chair, stood shakily on one foot.

"I can carry you down the stairs," he said.

"No, I'm fine," she said. Before she could chicken out, she dove into the clear water. It was heaven. She struck out for the infinity wall, hearing the splash as Tuareg joined her in the water.

Kicking hurt her ankle, so she used her arms to propel her along. When she reached the wall, she clung, shaking the water out of her eyes and dipping her head back to get the hair from her face.

"Are you all right?"

"I shouldn't kick with my injured leg, but this feels wonderful," she said, smiling as she met his gaze. His hair was slicked back, his dark eyes fathomless. He turned and began to swim laps. Lisa watched for a few moments, then let her gaze move around the setting and to the distant views. It was so pretty her heart ached.

When she was sufficiently refreshed, she leisurely swam to the steps and hopped up to the coping. Sitting on the edge, she let the sun warm her while her feet dangled in the water. Idly, she watched Tuareg swimming. He must have made a dozen laps but showed no signs of slowing down.

She memorized the day. She had a journal at the camp, had been keeping one for years. With no family, she had only her friends to share her life with and her constant travel made real closeness difficult to achieve. Sara and Bailey were her two best friends. She kept the journal for herself—when she was old and unable to travel, she'd have a wonderful life to look back on.

The last two days would be most memorable. She didn't want to forget a thing before she could write the events down. What happened and how she felt about everything. Especially her awareness of the man swimming like the hounds of hell were after him.

Tuareg continued to push himself. The mindlessness of swimming helped him to forget. The exercise drove the demons away and let him sleep at night. Not for long, but enough.

Taking another deep breath, he turned, kicked off from the wall and headed back along the lane. He caught a glimpse of Lisa sitting on the edge of the pool.

He had a guest. Responsibilities. Slowing, he changed directions and swam over to her.

He held on to the side and shook the water from his face. "Ready to leave?" he asked.

"Not yet. This is lovely. Do you swim competitively?"

"No."

"You could. With endurance like that, and your speed, you'd probably win events."

He frowned and grabbed the wall with both hands, leveraging himself out to sit beside her. Water streamed from his body. The sun felt warm on his skin. Nura had not been one for swimming. She preferred to sit in a lounger and recline in the sun. If it grew too hot, she'd move to the shade. Her hair didn't like the water, she'd often said. He missed her.

"I assume you get a lot of use from this pool. Isn't the weather always warm?" Lisa asked.

"For the most part. We do get cooler temperatures during the winter months. But even then, it's warmer than most of the rest of the world."

"Seattle is cool more often than warm. I don't often swim in an outdoor pool. The local community center has a great indoor one. But, of course, no view except for the concrete walls. I wonder why they never painted a mural on it. That would give the place some ambiance." She gestured to the distant mountains. "Something like this would be terrific."

"Perhaps you should suggest it when you return home," he said.

"Have you been to Seattle?" she asked.

"No. I have visited San Francisco and Los Angeles on your West Coast."

"Come up sometime, it's a great place. Nothing prettier than a clear day with the sun shining on Mount Rainier. Happens at least a couple of times a year," she joked.

He nodded. "Perhaps."

Why had he said that? He had no interest in traveling. It had lost its appeal for him three years ago. He'd gone with Nura to indulge her love for seeing new places, meeting new people, partying at new clubs. But it held no meaning for him without her. Yet he'd almost agreed to visit Seattle.

He shifted and Lisa looked at him. Her eyes were clear and direct; their gray color unusual. Sometimes they were almost smoky-blue, other times steely-gray. Could a person judge her mood by their color? Or was it the color of her clothes that caused the changes?

"I want to thank you for your hospitality. I really appreciate it. However, I think I need to get back to the dig. They're depending on me. I can still photograph the artifacts in the tent even if I'm seated. The work won't wait, it's piling up," she said.

"The doctor said to stay off your foot for a couple of days."

"I know, but the compound is small. I can easily get one of the team to help me get around. Once on a stool, I can sit all day."

"You can borrow the wheelchair if you like," he said. It wouldn't be the best solution, the ground was undoubtedly rough. But it would keep her mobile while protecting her foot. He could fly her to the camp and check out the place before leaving her.

But why should he care? He scarcely knew her.

Yet for the first time in years he was interested in something beside escaping to the desert. Her comments about the site had him curious about the artifacts they were uncovering. Was it a worthwhile excavation or only a delaying tactic for his project?

"That would be a great help, thank you," she said.

He glanced at her. She was gazing over the infinity edge of the pool to the distance far beyond. She had made no effort to flirt with him. For some reason that annoyed him. Even before Nura died, women used to flirt and hope—for what he wasn't sure, some betrayal on his part to his wife? That would never happen. He had loved Nura since they were children. No one else could ever compare.

He was not interested in trying to find a new woman. He had his memories. They'd had several years together as man and wife. Those memories would have to carry him to the grave.

"We'll leave in the morning. I'll fly the helicopter so you can get those pictures you wanted from the air," he said, banishing his thoughts of Nura and concentrating on the present.

Her delighted smile startled him. What would it take to have her look that way more often? Obviously more than wealth and position—which he had in abundance. She was an interesting mix of naive enthusiasm and cautious constraint.

In a way, they were alike—neither was willing to risk much to connect with others. It didn't sound as if she had memories like he had. But why should that concern him?

He scowled and rose, heading for one of the chairs and the towels that were folded there. Snatching one up, he rubbed his hair, trailing the towel down the rest of his body to capture the last of the moisture. He took a folded one and walked back to offer it her.

"Towel?"

She smiled and reached for it, wringing out her hair once more before drying it with the towel.

Nura would never have let her hair become a tangled mess, but Lisa didn't even seem to notice. The sun caught glints of pure gold in the strands, changing it from mousy brown to gleaming chestnut. Nothing like the inky black of his wife's hair. But pretty.

Lisa lay on her bed and looked at a magazine after her swim. Tuareg had tea sent to her room, with sweet cakes and dates. She sat near the window when eating them, after first photographing the elegant china and sterling-silver tea set. She also took pictures of her room. While she might include the tea service, she knew she wouldn't publish the images of the room, but she wanted them for her personal album—to remember a fairy-tale day in a beautiful home that was so sad.

The sooner she got back to work, the better. Before she allowed herself to dream dreams that would never be. Or become enamored with a man still in love with his dead wife.

CHAPTER FOUR

LISA LEANED AGAINST the window and watched the earth skim by below her the next morning. Tuareg had agreed to take her back to the camp in his helicopter. He'd flown higher when they first started, now he'd lowered the craft and was moving slowly. She could see the ambling river below, gleaming in the sunlight. Trees and shrubs grew in profusion near the banks. As the land spread out, however, there was less and less vegetation. The gorge it wound through would be relatively easy to dam and the plains were sloped enough to provide a wide basin for the reservoir.

She looked at the dusty tents in the distance, their destination. Soon she'd be back with her fellow excavation team members and her time with the exotic sheikh would come to an end. She smiled sadly, already feeling the tug of regret. It had been an amazing couple of days. But she knew she was better back on her own, without the lavish displays of wealth, without the beauty of a home that would never be hers enticing her to stop for a while and enjoy.

And without the tug of awareness that sprang up each time she looked at Tuareg.

She thought of the Frost poem—miles to go before she slept. Always in the back of her mind was the hope of meeting that one special man in the world. The one who wanted the same things she did—family, a home, roots and ties. So far she'd been wary of the men she knew who professed to want one or the other. None seemed to offer what she yearned for. Better to remain alone than risk everything and lose. At least that was Lisa's philosophy.

She began to take pictures of the site, the faint trail of the caravans still visible on the earth.

"Can you see that?" she asked, excited about the discovery.

"What?" Tuareg had given her the copilot's seat and provided headphones so they could hear each other above the din of the rotors. But she had been silent most of their short journey. Now she pointed.

"That trail there, see it? It's where the caravans crossed hundreds of years ago. It looks a lot like the ruts of the wagons which crossed into Oregon and California in America's great western migration. The earth is packed down so hard after hundreds of wagons, it doesn't grow vegetation. This trail looks the same. Can you follow it?" She was excited. Would Professor Sanders be as excited? Maybe he'd already seen this, but for Lisa, it was a first. No wonder the archeologists became excited over a discovery. This was heady stuff.

Tuareg slowly turned the helicopter and began following the faint trail. From the air it was clearly delineated, no vegetation grew on the path, even though clumps of desert plants could be seen scattered on both sides of it.

They traveled for some miles with Lisa taking a picture every few moments.

She looked up and smiled at Tuareg. "I don't know if the head of the team knows how clearly this is visible from the air. We could probably follow it on the ground and see if there were other camps. Has it been mapped?"

"I have no idea," Tuareg said. "Had enough?"

She looked longingly at the trail that seemed to go on to the horizon and reluctantly nodded. "Thank you, this has been fabulous!"

"You have an odd idea of what is fabulous," he commented as he turned back toward the archeological site. Any other woman he knew would have angled to stay longer—attend that party his mother had talked about. But Lisa had a strong sense of duty and was returning to the hardships of an archeological dig rather than stay in his comfortable home.

Once landed, they were met by several of the members of the group. The shortest seemed to be the one in charge.

"There's Professor Sanders. I hope he's not mad at me for pulling him away from the work. He's really captivated by what they're finding," Lisa said, fumbling with her seat belt.

Tuareg reached over and swiftly unbuckled the cumbersome clasp. The back of his hand brushed against her ribs, causing her to catch her breath. Lisa swallowed hard, gathering her senses. She'd been touched before and a lot more intimately than a casual brush of the back of a hand. But this was almost like a shock of electricity. The sooner she got back to normal, the better!

Tuareg hadn't noticed anything out of the ordinary, she noted. Thank goodness. She took a deep breath and prepared to scramble out of the seat, always conscious of her injured ankle. It felt better today. Maybe a few more days and she would be able to use it normally.

He glanced at the men and women waiting before reaching out to lift Lisa from her seat. She flung her arm around his neck, her face close to his. If she leaned closer, just a little, she could kiss him.

She groaned at her errant thoughts.

"Are you in pain?" he asked.

She nodded, closing her eyes. If he didn't put her down right now she was likely to do something too stupid to even think about.

"Hold on, I'll have you out in a second," he said. From the way he held her, she knew he did not feel the attraction that seemed to draw every bit of her consciousness into focus on him.

The door slid open and Tuareg engaged the stairs. They unfolded and he carried her down to the ground.

"If someone would get the wheelchair from the back, I'll put Lisa in it," he said to the group.

One of the young men ran up the stairs and appeared seconds later with the folded chair.

"I'm Tuareg," he said, lowering Lisa into the wheelchair when it had been opened and placed on the ground.

"Thank you for bringing her back," the shorter man said, reaching out to shake hands. "I'm Professor Sanders, head of this expedition. We've missed her. Our thanks to His Excellency for sending her back to us."

Lisa opened her mouth to correct the professor, but Tuareg's hand squeezed her shoulder and she closed her lips. Glancing at him quizzically, she wondered what he was doing.

Leaning close he said softly in her ear, "Let them

think I'm the pilot, that's true, after all, and it'll save trouble and explanations."

She nodded. She hadn't thought about it, but she supposed if the team knew who he was, they'd be fawning all over him or trying to convince him of the worth of the dig, get him to delay the dam for a few years. She could see both sides of the issue and was glad she wasn't the one to make the decisions. She turned to Professor Sanders to tell him about the trail.

He was as excited as she and couldn't wait to see her photographs.

"Do you develop here?" Tuareg asked.

"When it's dark. I only have a tent, so have to wait for full darkness."

"And not on the night of a full moon," one of the others chirped in.

Professor Sanders enjoyed having a visitor and quickly made sure Tuareg turned Lisa over to the care of one of the junior members so he could accompany him on a tour of the excavation. The professor proudly related all they'd discovered.

Lisa watched as Tuareg walked away.

"Hot," Jamie Farris said. She was one of the graduate students on the dig. Her long hair was always confined to a braid and she wore the dusty brown clothes that mingled so well with the sandy dirt. So no one could tell if she needed a change of clothes, she often joked.

Lisa nodded in agreement. Tuareg was definitely hot.

"Need help?" Paul asked, going to the back of Lisa's wheelchair and starting to push her toward the tents.

"This ground is hard going," she commented as she bumped along.

"Once it gets rolling, it's okay. The Jeep was delivered yesterday afternoon. I think it's running better than before you took it out."

"We have a pile of things recovered over the last two days. I've cataloged them and left them in order for the photos," Jamie said. She glanced again over her shoulder where Tuareg and Professor Sanders were deep in conversation. "You think he'll stay for a bit?"

"I have no idea," Lisa replied, resisting temptation to do her fair share of staring. She hoped he'd come to tell her goodbye, but didn't count on it. He would be glad to have his unwanted guest taken care of.

Looking around, nothing in camp appeared to have changed.

"Didn't the sandstorm cause any damage?" she asked.

"Didn't even get a stirring of air," Paul said.

"Which would have helped. I swear it was a hundred and twenty here yesterday," Jamie said.

Lisa kept quiet about swimming in the cool pool, but wondered how the storm had formed and bypassed the excavation.

Paul wheeled her into the large tent where the artifacts were housed. There were boxes already packed, sealed and labeled. Others stood empty awaiting new discoveries. Lisa's photography gear was kept in her tent, in specially designed cases that withstood sand, dust and moisture. One set of all photographs was sent to the university each week, another set was packaged with each box as it was packed. A third set was put into binders with the catalog pages of each artifact. There were several binders already compiled.

"How long before you can walk again?" Jamie asked.

"If it's only a sprain, I should be able to hobble

around in another day or two," she replied, already growing impatient with sitting in a wheelchair.

At least she'd have the work to do to keep her mind off her injury.

"I'll come get you for lunch," Paul said with a cheery smile. He waved and took off. None of the archeologists liked being away from the dig for long. Jamie was right behind him.

Silence settled in the tent. Lisa glanced around with resignation. It was the same as she'd left it, except for the increased number of items needing to be photographed. She pushed on the wheels, relieved to find she could propel herself on the hard-packed dirt. Soon she had her camera and close-up lenses and was absorbed in her work. Thoughts of a luxury villa forgotten.

Tuareg listened attentively to Professor Sanders. He'd seen Lisa disappear into a large tent near the center of the compound. He hoped the tour would end up there. She had not even looked back.

She both puzzled and intrigued him. He felt jaded to the wiles of women. Flirting was an art form in the circles he and Nura had traveled in. Yet Lisa had displayed none of the lures he expected. Her gaze was frank and forthright, her smile almost contagious. Every time she was delighted in something, her entire face seemed to light up. He hoped she smiled at him again before he left.

Surprised at his train of thought, he concentrated on what Professor Sanders had to say. The man had a passion for the work and brought it alive for Tuareg.

"Tell me more about how you can determine the age," Tuareg said.

The professor was obviously thrilled to have someone new to talk to. All his team members, except possibly Lisa, knew almost as much as he did. A new audience was a treat.

By the time the sun was directly overhead, Tuareg had had enough. He appreciated the history of Moquansaid as well as the next man. But he was not someone to live in the past. The people who had inhabited Wadi Hirum had long died and become dust. Their ways were not his.

Once they had descended into the wide trenches, marked by strings and cards with numbers, the air had grown close. No air circulated belowground.

"So you can see why we were excited by that find. It proves beyond any doubt the people living here had contact with China." The professor held a small porcelain figure in his hand.

"You found that today?" Tuareg asked. The small figurine was of classical Chinese design.

"No, no, two days ago. But it is so amazing, I wanted to keep it safe until Lisa could photograph it."

"How do you know it wasn't dropped here long after the Wadi had been abandoned?" Tuareg asked.

The professor beamed, as if Tuareg were a prize student. "Because it was buried in one of the pots. The age of the pot, and the dirt surrounding it, match the rest of the area. Isn't it beautiful? Of course, we have samples of the dirt and the pot itself which have to be tested. I believe one of your universities will be able to do that within the next few weeks. But I'm sure I am right." Professor Sanders gazed lovingly at the statue. "An amazing find. Of course it has rejuvenated everyone, we hope to find similar treasures."

"What else have you unearthed?" Tuareg asked as he gazed ahead at a series of square holes, each carefully labeled.

"Come to the holding tent and I'll show you some recent items. And Lisa has photographs of everything neatly put in binders."

Tuareg refused to admit to himself that was the end result of his query. He wanted to see her again before he left. What better place than where she worked? He could remember her there.

He frowned. He didn't need to remember her. She was a stranger whom he rescued. She was better and now back to her life. They would never need to meet again.

Unless he took her to his cousin's birthday party as his mother had suggested.

The sun must be frying his brains.

Stepping into the large tent a few moments later, Tuareg felt the temperature change once again. It was still warm, but the blazing sun's heat was muted.

Lisa sat by a table; her camera was on a stand and trained on a small shallow dish. She looked up when they entered.

"I wondered if I'd see you before you left," she said. "I wanted to make sure to thank you for coming to my rescue."

"I'm sure I've been keeping him from returning, but it's so refreshing to show someone new what we're doing," the professor said. "I told him about your binders of images, would you mind showing him the things we've already discovered?"

"Not at all."

The professor invited Tuareg to join them for lunch in a short time and left him to Lisa.

Tuareg walked around the tent, looking at the artifacts still displayed and at the boxes packed and ready for shipment.

"Not quite up to your tent," she murmured, glancing around. The utilitarian setting was suitable for the work at hand, but she couldn't help comparing it to the tent Tuareg had in the desert.

"More practical," he murmured, looking at the pieces on the long table. The binders were stacked at one end. He picked up one and leafed through the pages. The color shots were perfect, from different sides, top and bottom.

"Doesn't seem very creative," he said.

"That part's not. But it pays the bills. The creative shots are in my tent. They are not part of the project."

He moved along the table and pulled out a folder. The pictures in this one showed the various members of the team at work. One or two showed them lounging in the late afternoon on flimsy aluminum folding chairs. Their faces reflected the exhaustion that comes at the end of a long day, yet happiness clearly showed through.

"And these?"

"For a memory book," she said, already adjusting the camera for a close-up of the shallow dish.

"Memory book?" he asked, closing it to watch her at work.

"I thought everyone would like a memento of the project. These people aren't all from the same university. Once the project is over, we'll all go our separate ways. So I thought a memory book of the time we spent here would be welcome."

"You're doing it for everyone?"

"Same photos, just multiple copies. Doesn't take long."

He looked at the pictures. They were good. It made him more impatient for the delivery of her books that he'd ordered.

"I don't see any of you," he commented when almost halfway through the stack.

"Can't take ones of myself," she said.

He watched her until she was finished with the plate.

"Give me the camera and I'll take some of you at the table."

She looked up in surprise. "You will?"

"Don't you think for a complete memory book all the members of the team need to be included?"

"I guess." She looked at the camera, then shrugged. "If you want to, why not?"

She fiddled with the settings and then handed the camera to Tuareg. "Just look through the eye piece, focus by turning the lens piece and then press here."

He stepped back, framing her with the table and artifacts. Taking several different angles, he snapped the shots.

"How long before you know if they turned out?" he asked.

"I'll probably develop several rolls of film tonight. I'm anxious to see the ones I got from the air. So I'll know then."

He glanced at his watch. "When is your lunchtime?"

"Around noon. If you have to leave before, they'd understand. Thank you for bringing me back. And for everything."

Tuareg didn't need to be thanked. He returned the camera and turned. "I will have the doctor come here tomorrow to check your ankle." He could easily send the man with his pilot. But Tuareg would rather fly the craft himself.

"It's fine. I won't walk on it for another day or two and by then it'll be all right."

"I'll bring him here to double-check. And to see the pictures," he said again. Did she not want him to visit?

Her smile once against made her eyes almost blue.

Tuareg nodded and left. He wondered if pleasure made her eyes blue. If so, it was an indication she would not be displeased to have him return. Interesting thought.

Lisa listened as the helicopter started and then rose into the air. The sound faded slowly. He was gone. But he'd be back.

As soon as she finished dinner tonight, she'd develop the rolls of film. From the ruin, to the garden and tea setting at Tuareg's home, to the trail the caravans had taken, she hoped every shot came out.

Gazing off into space, she wished she'd taken one of Tuareg. When he'd been taking her picture today, she'd almost asked for one of him. Not that she needed one to remind her of the sexy man. She had every moment in his company committed to memory. When she was old and gray, she'd be able to tell anyone who would listen about her adventures with a genuine Arabian sheikh.

The afternoon flew by with the work that had piled up in her absence. Lisa was tired after dinner, but anxious to see the pictures she'd taken. It was a dark night. She made sure her tent was tightly closed. She had black material within the tent to create a dark room to ensure the film wouldn't be fogged. Slowly, she worked in the darkness, sure of the different stages of the process. Soon she could turn on the red light, courtesy of their portable generator. When the photos began to show on the paper, she was pleased. The quality was excellent. The ruins were amazing. She hoped she could get back there before she left the country.

The ones at Tuareg's home were equally good. There were so many places there she would have loved to photograph. But only with his permission.

Even the ones he took of her were good. He'd framed her at the work table, with enough background that everyone on the team would remember how that tent had looked.

She put the ones of the caravan trail aside to show Professor Sanders in the morning. Maybe he'd want to expand the site. Or even find another one of interest to research once Wadi Hirum was covered by water.

It was late when she went to bed. The cot couldn't compare with the luxurious bed she'd had at Tuareg's home. Or even the divan in the tent. She still felt sore in places, stiff. Her ankle gently throbbed, a reminder she'd done too much.

But all of it faded as she lay awake long after she thought she'd sleep. If Tuareg came tomorrow, it may be the last time she'd see him. The thought made her sad. Yet she couldn't come up with a single reason to meet with him again.

In the morning, Lisa was pleased to realize her ankle no longer ached as much as it had. Now it only felt stiff when she rotated it, nothing like the sharp pain the day she'd injured it. It was definitely healing.

She remembered Tuareg's holding her. And the flashback memories from her childhood. She shivered slightly. She'd never forget the night her mother died. She'd been alone for hours, calling, afraid. She would have been totally freaked out if she'd been alone in the sandstorm. Tuareg had no idea how much his being there had meant.

When she heard the helicopter later that morning Lisa wheeled the chair to the tent entrance and peered out. The machine landed light as a thistle. Dr. al Biminan came down the steps, followed by Tuareg. Her heart caught, then beat rapidly. She snuck her camera up and took a photo with the telephoto lens she'd put on earlier. She had to work fast before anyone realized what she was doing.

By the time Tuareg turned toward her, she had the camera back in her lap, changing the lens before he came close enough to suspect she had taken his picture. This was strictly for her—not for distribution.

Tuareg ignored the members of the team who were gathered nearby, walking directly toward her tent. He wore dark slacks and a white shirt, opened at the throat. The sleeves had been rolled up his forearm. He looked as if he were taking a quick break from a business meeting. Did he only wear the robes when staying in the desert?

She pushed the chair outside and watched as he walked purposefully. She could feel the pull of attraction. If her heart weren't racing, she felt she could almost make herself believe he was no more important to her than any other man.

The doctor hurried beside him.

"Good morning," Lisa called as they drew near. The day seemed suddenly brighter.

"How is your ankle?" Tuareg asked.

"Much better, thank you. I've been taking the anti-inflammatory medicine. I stood on it for a few moments today and it scarcely hurt."

Dr. al Biminan smiled a greeting and spoke to her through Tuareg.

"The doctor hopes it is better. He brought a support boot for you to wear until it is completely healed." Without another word, Tuareg went round to the back of the wheelchair and turned it to enter the tent.

The doctor completed his examination quickly, then fitted the padded boot on her leg and foot with Velcro fasteners. It gave support yet allowed mobility. Gingerly, Lisa rose to stand on it. She felt no discomfort beyond a dull ache.

The doctor told her not to overdo it.

"When I need to, I can walk. Thank you. I'll continue to favor my other ankle until it's completely healed," she promised, inclining her head slightly in acknowledgment.

Tuareg said something to the doctor who smiled, nodded and then turned to leave the tent.

"Are you leaving already?" Lisa asked.

"The doctor wants to check out the dig. There is growing interest in some sectors as news of the discoveries are conveyed to the capital. He told me of his interest, so I thought a brief tour would be in order. What new treasures have been uncovered since I was here?"

"Nothing exciting. I've taken photos of the porcelain figurine, however. Professor Sanders said you'd seen it. Isn't it exquisite?" Lisa pulled a photo from the stack she was working on. She'd developed them among the others last night and was still writing the information on each artifact for the catalog.

"Very beautiful," he murmured, studying the figurine in the picture.

"My mother enjoyed meeting you," he said a moment later, laying down the photograph. He withdrew a small envelope from his pocket and held it out to Lisa.

Lisa opened it. The short note was in English,

inviting her to spend the weekend with Yasmin al Shaldor and reminding her of the party for her niece.

She looked up at Tuareg.

"She's inviting me to visit this weekend."

His eyes narrowed slightly. "Indeed?"

She held the note out to him.

He took it and quickly scanned it, then handed it back. His demeanor seemed to undergo a slight change. He seemed a bit more reserved. "If you accept, I can arrange to have the helicopter pick you up."

Lisa reread the note, surprised at the invitation yet puzzled by Tuareg's reaction. She'd enjoyed talking with Yasmin, but had considered it merely a polite interlude with a stranger. She had never expected to hear from Tuareg's mother again or receive an invitation to stay with her.

She eyed him for a moment, trying to figure out what had changed.

"I would love to go," she said. "Except—does she realize our attire is geared for the dig? I don't have any suitable clothes. I don't think I can attend your cousin's party."

"Do not concern yourself. My mother will understand. For her place, you have the dress you wore at the villa," he said, referring to the dress he'd provided.

"If that's enough," she said doubtfully. The dress his mother had worn the other day was definitely a couturier creation. Still, Yasmin had to know Lisa had come to work on an excavation and would not expect her to have a wide assortment of clothes.

She looked up into Tuareg's dark eyes. He was studying her closely. When she met his gaze, he looked away, picked up a small shard of pottery. "Part of a bowl?"

She nodded.

He replaced it carefully on the table.

"So you will go?" he asked.

"Yes. Please thank your mother for me. Will you be there?"

"No. When not at the desert, I stay at my villa. It is a short ride into the city. My mother has a place in a high-rise in the heart of Soluddai. Much more convenient for her when my father is traveling. They also have a home near mine."

"So we'll be at the apartment in the city?" she asked.

"Yes. The party will be close by. I need to return. I will send the helicopter for you on Friday at two. Will your duties permit you to leave by then?" Tuareg asked.

"I'll make sure I'm caught up by then," Lisa said. She was trying to gauge if he was displeased with her acceptance of his mother's invitation or not. Should she not have accepted?

He held out his hand for hers. Surprised, Lisa put hers in his.

"Come, see how you walk in that device. Once I know you'll be all right, we'll leave." He helped her to rise.

She walked around the tent, perfectly capable of managing on her own, yet her hand clung to Tuareg's. He seemed in no hurry to let her go.

"Have you been back to the desert?" she asked.

"Not yet. I will go again soon."

"It was so lovely. I hope to resume my explorations once I'm fit again," she said. "And if Professor Sanders will trust me with the Jeep."

"It is dangerous to go off alone," he said.

"You were living there alone."

"That's different, I'm familiar with the desert," he said.

"I'm learning. Now I know to take a thick cloth in case of sandstorm, make sure I have lots of water if I get stuck somewhere. And it wouldn't hurt to have a shortwave radio, but the camp only has a couple and I'm not high on the list to have one."

"The desert can be a ruthless place. Unforgiving."

"Yet you love it," she said softly.

He didn't reply, but sought the view from the open tent flap. It was as if the land called to him, grounded him.

"If you didn't go back to the desert, what have you been doing besides ferrying me around?" she asked, returning to the wheelchair.

He glanced at her. "This and that."

"Planning on the dam?"

"That is taken care of by engineers."

"And what did you study in university?"

"Mechanical engineering. I have had input on the dam."

"And on how to erect your tent so the sandstorm didn't blow it to the next country," she said. "What else do you do?"

"As in?"

"Do you have a job, go to work every day? Though I guess if you can take time off to fly people around in your helicopter, you don't have a regular nine-to-five job."

"I have offices in the central city. Most of my work is special projects for my uncle," Tuareg said. "And only recently. Before that, Nura loved to travel and we spent more time out of the country than here. You would have called us unofficial ambassadors for Moquansaid. At least that is what Nura often said. She loved Europe."

"Really? But this is such a cool place," Lisa said, surprised.

* * *

Tuareg stood in the opening of the tent, frowning slightly. It was an innocuous question. Yet it had him wondering not for the first time why Nura preferred to spend more time away from home than in it. She'd been given free rein in decorating the house he'd bought after they were married. Of course, she insisted she needed to travel to Paris and London to actually see the items she wanted—rich brocades and delicate lace, antique furnishings. But once the decoration had been completed, she had no desire to spend much time in the house.

Nor did she like the desert.

She preferred parties and shopping for new dresses and jewelry. Activities that kept her always on the move.

He looked at Lisa, her enthusiasm was genuine. She'd been fascinated by his tent, by the grounds at the villa, by the sights she'd seen from the air. Even about finding the tracks of the long-ago caravans. What was it about her that found the mundane intriguing? Was it the novelty? Or would she be just as enthusiastic in another ten years, fifty years?

He suspected the latter. She seemed to be someone who liked finding out how things worked, what caused events, about remnants of the past.

Tuareg wanted to leave. He'd done his duty, brought the doctor, given his mother's note. He'd thought it would be just a polite letter after meeting Lisa at his home. The invitation caught him by surprise.

He had thought today would be the last time he'd see her. Being around Lisa had him feeling emotions he'd thought long gone. Nura was dead. She had been his love since they were teenagers. He'd had three years to get over her death, but still felt her loss as strongly as that first day. No one could ever take her place.

So why did he think about brushing his fingers through Lisa's hair? He did not need to know if it was as silky soft as it looked. Why did he want to be with her when she went to the capital to photograph the old buildings? There were many others who could make sure she saw the best of the architecture. Why was he thinking of taking her back to his tent, sharing his special place with a stranger? That was his special haven. Even Nura had never gone there with him. Lisa was nothing like Nura.

The sooner he bid her farewell, the better.

"I'll send the helicopter on Friday," he said. Without another word, he headed for the craft. He needed to get away.

She was not beautiful as Nura had been with her height and sleek sophistication. Nura's dark hair had glowed in sunshine and candlelight. Lisa was not as tall, but more rounded. Her sunny disposition had him thinking more along the lines of…of…of a puppy than a sexy woman.

Not true. He didn't want to brush his fingers through a puppy's fur. Didn't want to see a puppy's reaction to the desert. Or listen to one talk excitedly about new experiences. Or try to determine exactly what made a puppy's eyes change color.

Dr. al Biminan saw him and hurried to join him. As Tuareg started the engines he glanced toward the large tent housing the artifacts. Lisa stood in the doorway. He couldn't see her clearly at the distance, but knew she was watching him. For an odd moment, he felt a lift in his heart.

CHAPTER FIVE

BY TWO O'CLOCK ON FRIDAY, Lisa was a nervous wreck. She had packed the nicest clothes she'd brought but she knew they would not be suitable for anything but the most casual visiting. Surely his mother realized that. Her note had said her husband was out of town and she'd love company for the weekend. Maybe she just wanted the novelty of learning more about Seattle and Lisa's work on the dig and they'd spend the time inside talking or sitting on a patio. Did the high-rise apartments in the city have terraces?

She heard the helicopter long before she saw it. She doubled-checked her tote. She had clothes, makeup and her journal. She'd caught up on her daily entries since she'd returned and knew she'd have lots of new experiences to capture. Her camera bag sat beside the tote. Unless invited to, she would not presume to photograph Yasmin's home. But if they went for a drive or something, she wanted to be prepared. She also packed a copy of the site's memory book, to share the excavation with her hostess.

Professor Sanders joined her to watch the white craft land. The golden lettering gleamed in the sunshine.

"You'll be back on Sunday, right?" he asked.

"Yes, professor. Shall I bring you back anything from civilization?" she asked. The man had a weakness for ice cream and lamented many evenings how he missed it.

"Only some ice cream, if you can," he replied, smiling at the absurdity. They had no way to keep food frozen.

The man who climbed down from the craft when it was stopped was unfamiliar to Lisa. She felt an immediate pang of disappointment that Tuareg hadn't come for her. He was undoubtedly too busy to ferry his mother's guest. Lisa lifted her things and headed toward the helicopter.

"Don't get used to city lights," the professor called after her.

Lisa shook her head. She was growing to love her work and became almost as excited as the archeologists when new finds surfaced. Maybe she'd try for another dig when they finished. Next summer she could be in the wilds of Mexico or the deep jungle of South America. She liked the quiet of the desert, the feeling of living closer to the earth, the discovery of lost people and how they lived.

But it was fun to take off for a day and soar above it all. How astonished ancient civilizations would be to see this helicopter.

"Hello. Lisa Sullinger?" the pilot asked, reaching for her tote.

"Yes. That's right."

"His Excellency gave instructions to fly you to his mother's home." He showed her to the stairs and stood aside as she climbed inside. She soon sat in one of the seats on the far side, next to a window.

The pilot went to the front. "His Excellency also said

you'd be interested in seeing some of the land from the air and to fly south for a short distance."

"Wonderful. The professor was quite excited about the shots I got last time," she said, already reaching for her camera. "I'm looking for trails where caravans moved generations ago."

The pilot quickly started the engines and soon had the helicopter rising above the camp and heading south. Lisa watched from the window, searching for the packed earth, her gaze skimming across the barren ground. She refused to acknowledge even to herself that she'd much rather Tuareg had come to get her. She focused on the task at hand, excited to find the faint wandering path a moment later. Caught up in taking pictures, she soon forgot her disappointment.

A half hour later, the pilot turned the craft toward the northwest and flew straight. Lisa settled back in her seat, gazing ahead as the capital city drew closer. From a mere smudge on the horizon until she could see the windows in the buildings, it drew closer and closer. The pilot flew to the limits of the city, then turned slightly, circumventing the space, talking constantly with ground control in Arabic. Finally, he turned left and moved to hover over a tall building. Slowly he settled on the roof. Two guards in uniform stood near the door to the stairs.

The high-rise building was near the heart of the downtown area of Soluddai. Other tall buildings surrounded the one they landed on. The engines were shut down and silence descended.

"One of the guards will escort you to Madame al Shaldor's apartment," he said, opening the door and extending the stairs.

"Thank you for a most enjoyable flight," she said,

gathering her things. She'd seen traces of the caravan tracks and caught a glimpse of the gorge where the dam would be built. The pilot took her tote and camera bag, handing them to one of the men who stood at the bottom of the stairs.

The elevator was quiet as it descended only a few levels before stopping and opening to a small hallway. There was only one door. Lisa realized Yasmin and her husband must occupy the entire floor. The uniformed guard knocked. A maid opened the door and ushered them inside. The man placed the tote and camera bag on the floor inside the door and left.

"Welcome. Madame is in the salon. Please." The maid led the way.

The apartment was huge. Lisa saw lovely inlaid tile and parquet floors as she quickly followed the maid. Soon they entered a sunny room with yellow silk walls and beautiful windows framing a view of the city.

Yasmin rose from her sofa and crossed to greet Lisa.

"I'm so delighted you accepted my invitation," she said. She smiled warmly at Lisa and gestured for her to sit on the sofa.

"I have called for tea. A delightful custom from the British. How is your ankle? Tuareg said the doctor pronounced it healing."

"It's so much better than the other day." Lisa showed off the dark blue boot she wore. "This enables me to walk with very little discomfort. I didn't appreciate mobility until I lost it."

The maid came in carrying a silver tray loaded with a heavy silver teapot, fine china cups and saucers and a delectable assortment of finger sandwiches and scones.

"It looks wonderful," Lisa said in appreciation.

"One of the pleasures of traveling, picking up customs from other locations and making them part of my own. I also like popcorn when watching a movie, which I started after a visit to America," Yasmin said with a smile.

Lisa laughed. "A very fine tradition."

"Tell me how you managed this week with your foot injured."

Lisa asked if she could have someone fetch her camera bag. Before long she was explaining how things worked at the excavation, sharing the photographs she'd brought and enjoying a delicious cream tea as if they were in the heart of London.

By the next evening Lisa felt as comfortable with Yasmin as she did with most people. The woman had been beyond gracious in making her feel welcomed. The food was to her liking and the discussion lively and delightful. Yasmin had traveled extensively, primarily to Europe, but she had also been to New York twice. Lisa loved hearing her talk about shopping in some of New York's exclusive boutiques.

Yasmin had prevailed on Lisa to attend the birthday party of her niece. When Lisa had protested that she had no proper clothes, Yasmin arranged a fast shopping trip. Lisa insisted on buying her own dress, much to Yasmin's dismay.

"I love buying clothes, for me, my daughters, nieces. Do let me," Yasmin had cajoled.

But Lisa had been adamant.

She was pleased with the deep rose color, the simple lines and the flattering fit of the gown she'd found. It had cost more, even with the exchange rate, than she would have spent at home. But she didn't want to disgrace herself with her hostess. She found some comfortable, low-heeled shoes to wear that did not hurt her ankle. She refused to wear the boot to a party. She planned to sit as much as possible.

Lisa had offered to take a small camera to photograph the birthday girl and provide a memento of the party as her gift. Yasmin was pleased with the suggestion. They agreed on a time to meet in the salon just prior to Tuareg's arrival. Her son would escort them to the event.

As the time drew near for Tuareg to pick them up, Lisa's nervousness rose. She was unsure if she should be attending. She didn't speak Arabic and doubted most of the people spoke English. Still, she'd mainly be on the sidelines and would enjoy seeing how the young woman's birthday was celebrated.

Yasmin looked almost as nervous as Lisa felt when Lisa joined her in the salon. Did she not like large gatherings?

"I do hope he comes," Yasmin murmured.

"Who?" Lisa asked.

"Tuareg. He hasn't been to any family gathering since Nura died. He said he'd escort us to this event, but I'm worried he'll cancel at the last moment."

"Was her death recent?" Lisa asked. She knew so little about the man and his past.

"Three years ago. Such a tragedy. They were a perfect couple. Both tall and slender. She had so much energy. Always on the go. She loved to throw parties and attend them. She would have made a big to-do about tonight's. There was never anyone else for either of them." Yasmin sighed slightly, looking sad.

"How did she die?" Lisa asked.

"Aneurysm. Totally unexpected. Suddenly she

screamed in pain, clutched her head and collapsed. Moments later she died. We were stunned. She was only thirty."

Older than Lisa was, but only by a year. "How tragic," she murmured. The woman should have had an entire life still ahead of her. "They had no children?" she asked. Much as she'd hate to be widowed, it would seem to make things easier if children were there to comfort her. Her father had told her she made it bearable after his wife died. Only—he'd died too soon himself. There'd been no one for Lisa after that.

"No children. Nura had too much fun traveling to settle down. I suppose eventually they would have had one or two. Now I will never have a grandchild from Tuareg. There is a picture of her on the table there. The children they would have had—beautiful."

Lisa rose and crossed to the table near the far corner. An enlarged snapshot showed a beautiful woman laughing into the camera, an attentive Tuareg beside her.

"He might marry again," Lisa said. Nura had been beautiful. Her dark looks dramatic, her eyes flashing fire and excitement. For a moment Lisa wished she could have met her, photographed her. Captured that beauty herself on film.

Yasmin shook her head sadly. "There could never be a woman who would capture his heart like Nura. I have other children and I hope they will all bless me with grandchildren. But not Tuareg."

Lisa frowned. The statement sounded melodramatic. The man she knew wasn't going to pine away the rest of his life. He was too virile and dynamic to grieve forever. One day he'd find someone as spectacular as this woman had been and fall in love all over again. She put the picture down just as the door opened and Tuareg stepped inside.

He caught the movement from his eye and turned, narrowing his gaze when he saw what Lisa had been staring at. She could read nothing from his expression.

"Tuareg, we were just wondering when we might see you." Yasmin rose. "We are ready. Lisa has offered to photograph the party and give the pictures to Jeppa as her gift."

"Then my cousin will be double lucky. I have one of Lisa's books as a gift," he said.

"You do?" she asked in surprise.

"The one with children and playgrounds," he replied.

She was touched he thought enough of her work to make such a gesture.

The limousine waiting for them was sumptuous. Lisa felt as if she were living a fairy-tale weekend. Would she end up without a slipper and have it all vanish in an instant?

In a short time they arrived at the home of Tuareg's uncle. As she walked up the wide sidewalk, Lisa wished she could begin taking pictures. The guests ran the gamut, from young and trendy to elderly and conservative. Laughter seemed the key for the night, no matter what age.

Inside she was treated to a beautiful setting. Lights glowed everywhere. The jewelry and shimmery fabrics of the ladies added to the sparkle. The men were handsome in their dark suits. It seemed everyone was in western attire. She was surprised at first. She had expected Arabian garb. It took several minutes for their small party to work their way across the entryway to greet Tuareg's cousin.

When they reached her, Jeppa did a double take when

she spotted Tuareg. Quickly she threw herself into his arms and hugged him, jabbering away a mile a minute. Lisa wished she understood what the girl was saying, but it was obvious she was happy to see Tuareg. Lisa drew her camera from her small purse and snapped a quick shot. A moment later Tuareg untangled himself from his cousin's embrace and switched to English as his cousin greeted her aunt.

"Jeppa, my mother's guest, Lisa Sullinger. My cousin Jeppa."

"Happy birthday, Jeppa," Lisa said. "I hope it's all right that I came."

"Of course. I'm happy to meet you." She laughed and hugged Tuareg's arm. "I'm so happy to have you here! A gift indeed for my birthday. Tante Yasmin," and then she switched back to Arabic.

"Come, I'll see you have something to drink. And introduce you to some other family members," Tuareg said a moment later, guiding Lisa away from his exuberant cousin.

It seemed as if Tuareg knew everyone there. He introduced Lisa to a couple standing near one of the tall windows, mentioning she worked at the Wadi Hirum excavations. It was a good icebreaker. Everyone seemed interested in learning about the dig. Another young man joined the group, then two elderly women—sisters, Lisa thought. From time to time, glances were exchanged between the people. Lisa tried to interpret what they meant, but she hadn't a clue. Was it awkward to have her at a gathering of family and long-term friends?

Tuareg made sure she was introduced to more guests. When she had a chance, she stepped back a little bit and lifted her small camera. "I do need to take photographs or I won't have any for Jeppa," she said. "I can manage myself if you wish to chat to friends." Her ankle was starting to bother her again. She'd have to find a chair and rest it.

"Tell me what you wish to take," Tuareg said.

"Would it be rude to just wander around and snap candid shots?" she asked.

"Not at all. Lead on."

"I'll be fine. You go talk to your friends." She looked around, people seemed to be staring at them.

He glanced briefly toward a group, then back to Lisa. "I've spoken to all I wish to."

"Oh." She was momentarily taken aback. But she wanted to give her hostess a memory book, so began to study the crowd, soon lost in framing shots and trying for different angles that would add interest to a picture.

When she had taken photos of a sufficient number of the guests, she worked her way toward Jeppa. The guest of honor should definitely be included.

She had just raised the camera when a man stepped in front of her and yanked it from her hands.

"Hey," she said.

Tuareg stepped closer and spoke quickly to the man. He hesitated a moment, then with a slight bow, returned the camera. His gaze never left Lisa, however.

She checked the camera, it was undamaged.

"A camera-phobe?" she murmured, glaring at him.

"No, simply making sure unwanted photographs aren't taken. I explained you were with me, and taking pictures with full knowledge of the family."

"Including Jeppa?" she asked, dismayed her surprise had been blown.

"No. If she notices, she'll think little about it. Continue."

Lisa smiled at the command. He did it without thinking. "Yes, sir."

She took several good photographs of Jeppa, one of her dancing with her father, another of her laughing with friends. And one with Yasmin.

"Go stand by her and I'll get you both," she told Tuareg.

"Not this time," Tuareg said absently. He looked over the people dancing, the laughing crowd near the opened windows. He knew most of the people here, but had little to say to them. The mindless chatter seemed to ebb and flow like the sea. Nura would have loved it, greeting everyone, exchanging gossip and planning new parties. The appeal had lost its excitement for him long ago, though he'd continued to please her. Now that she was no longer with him, he'd just as soon spend time with his plans for changing a portion of the desert to a fertile irrigated plain.

"Then, perhaps we could sit over there. I hate to admit my foot is bothering me," Lisa said.

"You should have said something earlier," he said, taking her elbow in his palm and guiding her to one of the small alcoves. Empty chairs lined most of the area. The elderly sisters they'd talked with earlier were sitting near one edge. Tuareg deliberately chose the far side. He didn't want to get into conversations with friends.

Once Lisa sat down, he looked at her ankle.

"It aches, but I'll be fine. It was just the constant standing," she said, reaching down to rub it a little.

"Would you like to return home?" he asked.

She glanced at him. "So soon?"

He almost smiled. "I was ready to leave about two hours ago."

"What about your mother?"

"I'll find her and see if she wishes to leave now or have me send back the car."

"It seems a bit rude to leave so early."

"I've had enough. I suspect you have as well. With your ankle, you have a perfect excuse without offending anyone. Wait here, I won't be long."

He strode through the crowd, glad for the excuse to leave. Finding his mother, he made sure she had a ride home since she wished to stay longer. He went to his cousin, wishing her happy birthday once more and telling her they were leaving.

She smiled happily. "I'm glad you came. I enjoyed meeting your friend," she said with a look over toward Lisa.

He wondered what fantasies she was conjuring up. For a moment he almost set the record straight. But to give voice to it gave it more credence than warranted.

"I can't wait to get to know her better," Jeppa said. "I know it was hard, the first party without Nura. We all miss her," she continued. "I'm glad you've found someone else to spend time with."

"She is my mother's guest," Tuareg said tightly. Maybe he should set the record straight before Jeppa spread rumors to the contrary.

Jeppa laughed. "Of course, it would not be right to have her staying at your home with no chaperone. Your mother is doing it correctly."

Tuareg give his cousin a kiss on her cheek and turned to leave. Jeppa confirmed what he'd suspected when he first saw the note from his mother to Lisa. Was she matchmaking? His father was in Paris on business. Would he have interfered had he been home?

Tuareg crossed the room back to Lisa, ignoring the people who spoke to him. The sooner he got things cleared up, the better. Was Lisa in on the plans?

Lisa smiled at him when he reached her. Tuareg could see the strain around her eyes, however.

His confrontation would have to wait. She was not feeling well.

"Ready?" he asked.

"Yes, thank you. The longer I sit, the harder it will be to get up," she said, rising to her feet. She stood for a moment as if bracing herself, then stepped away from the chair.

He could see her limp as they moved slowly to the front doors.

"Shall I carry you?" he asked.

"Good grief, no. How embarrassing that would be."

Yet the perfect opportunity to link them together. Maybe this bout of matchmaking was only on his mother's part.

Or maybe he was imagining everything.

The limo deposited them at his mother's building a short time later. He rode up the elevator silently. He had a key, would let Lisa in and then leave.

"Are you enjoying your stay?" he asked as the elevator reached the floor.

"Very much. Your mother and I went shopping today. It was quite an experience. Then she kindly drove me around the city so I could get an idea of what I want to take pictures of before I leave at the end of the summer. I would have snapped some shots today, but didn't have my best camera. It's such a lovely city."

He stepped into the lobby and unlocked the door to

the apartment. Standing aside for Lisa, he followed her inside. She was limping more now than before. Lights were on in the entryway, but the rest of the apartment was dark. As if in agreement, they walked toward the salon.

"Oh, wow," Lisa said softly when they reached the archway. The wall of windows gave way to the lights sparkling in the capital city. The black of night was the perfect backdrop to the blaze of lights from office buildings, streetlights and homes.

"Don't turn on the lights," she said, moving across the wide room to stand by the windows. "This is spectacular." For a long moment she stared. Tuareg looked at the colorful scene.

"I wish I'd brought my other camera. The one I have wouldn't capture this view. It's so lovely."

Tuareg came to stand next to her. "You have lights in Seattle," he commented.

"Sure, and if I come into a room where I can see them unexpectedly, I'm just as taken. Isn't it pretty?"

She glanced at him when he didn't respond. He looked out the window but she wasn't sure he saw the lights as she did.

"Tuareg?"

He looked at her. "What?"

"I'm glad you rescued me from the sandstorm and introduced me to your mother."

"Fate."

"Maybe. Anyway, I had a nice time tonight. I didn't think I would."

"Why is that?"

"I don't speak the language and don't usually move in such circles."

He glanced at her then looked back out the window.

It was easier to remember she was merely his mother's guest when he wasn't looking at her.

Her eyes were dark and mysterious in the faint light from the cityscape. Her hair as dark as Nura's. For a moment, he wished they'd met in another life, another time.

"Such circles?"

"Mmm, sheikhs are Arabian royalty, right? I'm used to regular people."

"We are regular. You make it sound as if we're some exotic species," he said, now trying to see her better in the faint illumination.

Lisa shrugged. To her, Tuareg was exotic, but not because of his title, more because of his heritage. He was a handsome man, strong enough to lift her with little effort. Able to take care of himself and others. A worldly traveler, representing his country to other countries. And a caring man, trying to change the lives of nomads and offer a better way for them. Yet there was a solitude that seemed out of place. Not the self-sufficiency he evidenced, but the feeling he was apart from his friends and family.

Lisa continued to stare out the window, but instead of enjoying the lights, she was remembering being in Tuareg's arms, being held tightly while the wind raged around them. If she closed her eyes, she could still smell the male scent unique to him. Almost feel the steely strength of his arms, holding her securely against the ravages of nature. It had been a scary event, yet she had not felt afraid. He could make anyone feel safe.

Snapping her eyes open, she stepped away. A polite good-night and she would escape to her bedroom.

He reached out to stop her from moving away. Turning her slowly, he looked into her eyes, his dark and un-readable.

"I loved my wife very much," he said. "I'm not looking for another."

Lisa blinked. Where had that come from?

"Okay," she said.

"So if you think my mother is arranging things to-ward that end, rest assured it is not with my knowledge or permission."

"I never thought any such thing! You mean you think your mother would try matchmaking?"

"She's happy being married, she would like to see me happy again," he said simply.

"Well, she needs to understand you make yourself happy. And she's probably happy being married to your father. Not just being married." She pulled her arm away from his hand.

"Maybe we should say goodbye now and relieve your mind of any worries that I have designs," she said, stung by his suggestion. "I can hire a car or some-thing to get back to the dig. I don't need anything further from you!"

"Perhaps designs is too strong? Maybe you just want to see what develops?"

"And why should anything develop?" she asked. "You kindly rescued me from a fall and the sandstorm. Now I'm better and we don't have any reason to see each other again. I shall thank your mother for her hos-pitality and return to camp. If she tries for any further contact, I'll plead too much work. That should protect you for any matchmaking endeavors."

He could tell Lisa was angry. He had meant to clear the air, not make her upset.

"My mother thinks she's helping me. She's worried that I haven't recovered from my wife's death."

"She knows you love your wife. But she said she doesn't expect you to marry again. I think you're imagining things."

"Even Jeppa thought that," he defended.

"I can't help what your cousin thinks. Thank you for bringing me back here. I need to get to bed and get off this ankle. Good night."

He studied her in the faint light from the window.

"I will always love Nura."

"There you are, then. No woman wants to come in second best—especially against a ghost who can do no wrong. Good night, Tuareg." She turned but once again he reached out to stop her flight.

The bright glare of light suddenly snapped on flooded the room. Lisa blinked at the brilliance and turned toward the door. One of Yasmin's maids stood on the threshold, looking startled. She said something in Arabic and bowed, backing away.

Tuareg called after her, crossing the room and speaking rapidly.

Lisa took a moment to get control of her emotions. How dare he suggest that she might have designs on him when it was his mother who had invited her. And she'd been careful at every encounter not to let her hopes rise. She knew he was so far from her realm that the most they'd ever be was cordial acquaintances. She was glad for the interruption.

She walked to the doorway, head held high.

Giving Tuareg and the maid a wide berth, she mumbled good night and fled down the hall to the room she was using. Tuareg called her name, but Lisa kept walking. Only when the door was safely shut behind her did she breathe again.

"Lisa?" He knocked on the door.

"Go away." She turned to face the door, half expecting him to barge in.

"I wanted to apologize if I was in error."

"Apology accepted. And you were. Good night."

"If you would let me explain."

"There's nothing to explain. Let's not make more of this than we already have." She waited, straining to hear any sound from the other side of the door. Endless moments ticked by. The silence grew. Sheikhs didn't fall for photographers from Seattle. Especially not rounded women with freckles across their noses, no family and not much sophistication. She knew that. She didn't need him telling her in so many words.

CHAPTER SIX

LISA GREETED HER HOSTESS the next morning with some reservation. She couldn't help wonder if Tuareg's assessment of his mother's offer of friendship had some merit. Why else would a woman a generation older befriend her? They had little in common, though Lisa had enjoyed her visit and found his mother charming and a delightful hostess.

Soon after Lisa was seated at the dining table, the maid entered carrying a tray of hot chocolate and hot coffee, which Yasmin then served, as well as fresh fruit and croissants. Lisa knew she could quickly get used to such luxury.

"I need to return to the dig earlier than expected," she said, hoping Yasmin wouldn't ask why.

"Oh dear, I thought we might go visit one of my dearest friends this afternoon."

"It would have been lovely, I'm sure, but the work at the site continues. We're up against a firm deadline and I need to do my fair share. Also, the sooner I can develop the pictures I took last night the sooner I can get the memory book to Jeppa."

Though how she was going to get the book to Jeppa

was unclear. Lisa would get her address and hope she could post it through the weekly pickup at the excavation.

"Stay until after lunch and I'll make sure someone takes you back if you must leave," Yasmin urged.

Lisa smiled and nodded, her heart beating faster when she thought about Yasmin calling Tuareg to arrange for the helicopter. It would take a couple of hours driving, but Lisa preferred that to being in Tuareg's debt for another trip. Or have him think it was a ploy to capture his attention.

He'd made it abundantly clear last night where his heart lay.

She nibbled on her croissant, wishing she had more of an appetite, but the thought of seeing Tuareg again had her on edge. Surely she could pretend nothing had happened and treat him casually as before. She had done nothing wrong. She wasn't matchmaking. And she didn't believe his mother was, either.

"How did you enjoy Jeppa's party?" Yasmin asked.

Glad for a safe topic, Lisa replied readily. Before long her concerns faded and she began to enjoy Yasmin's company again. The older woman was generous in sharing tidbits about the different relatives at the party. Lisa didn't remember half of the people she spoke of, but enjoyed the vignettes of each.

The time fled and before she knew it, Lisa heard the now familiar sound of the helicopter. She had her tote and camera bag by the front door. She was again wearing the jeans and long-sleeved shirt she'd arrived in, arms rolled up for coolness. And the support boot.

When Yasmin heard the knock at the door, she looked expectantly toward the entryway. Tuareg entered a moment later. His gaze went immediately to Lisa. She smiled self-consciously and glanced away, her heart pounding. Figured the one time she'd hoped he would send his pilot, he had to come himself.

Goodbyes were quickly said. Two minutes later Lisa stepped inside the helicopter. The man who had flown her in on Friday sat in the pilot's seat. Lisa sat where she had before. Tuareg sat in the copilot's seat, glancing around to make sure she fastened her seat belt.

He'd scarcely said three words to her, she thought, looking out the window, ignoring the pull of attraction that had her yearning to gaze at him throughout the flight. What would it be like to have his mother really be trying to foster a relationship between them?

Would Tuareg take her on an actual date? Not a visit to a family gathering, but to dinner, maybe dancing. She'd love to be swept around a club to some soft dreamy music, if she were held in Tuareg's arms.

The city gleamed in the afternoon sunshine, the white of the buildings almost hurting her eyes. Slowly, the helicopter rose and she pressed against the window for a final look when the craft turned and headed for the excavation site. She sat only feet from the man who had accused her of being part of a conspiracy to capture his heart.

Or, no, he had never put it quite like that, but that's what Lisa would want if she ever fell in love. Complete devotion from the man she loved. And Tuareg had made it clear Nura had been the love of his life.

Her indignation to his accusations gave way as the flight continued. She rotated her ankle, feeling it ache again. Standing last night had not been the best thing to do.

When they landed at the camp, Tuareg went down the stairs first and turned to offer his hand to Lisa. She put hers in his, feeling a jolt of awareness. Her glance flickered to his. His dark eyes watched her.

Licking suddenly dry lips, as she reached the ground, Lisa pulled her hand away. The pilot handed out her tote and camera case, which Tuareg snared. "I'll walk you to your tent," he said.

"I can manage," she said, holding out her hand for her bags. "I wouldn't want you to get the wrong impression."

He ignored her and gestured toward the center of the camp. "Go."

Suppressing a sigh, she gave in. It wasn't worth making an issue of it.

The others in the expedition were lounging around as it was Sunday afternoon. Several waved as Tuareg and Lisa passed, but no one rose to join them.

It was hot. No air stirred. The shade was limited to that made by tents and canopies. Tuareg stopped at her tent and handed her the bags. Glancing around, he leaned closer and spoke softly,

"I hope you have accepted my apology."

"Of course. It was simply a misunderstanding," she said. She couldn't help remembering how much more comfortable she'd been around him before, despite his being a sheikh. The party last night and his accusation after it had shown her what a fantasy world she'd been living in. She had better keep a good head on her shoulders.

But it was difficult with his face so close. By barely moving two inches, she could brush her lips against his jaw. Would he respond with a real kiss?

"Goodbye. Thank you for the ride." She jerked back and lifted the flap. Escape was uppermost in her mind. Head held high, Lisa held out her hands for her tote and camera case.

* * *

Tuareg knew he'd been dismissed. For a moment he was startled. It was an unusual experience for him. Nura would have called him spoiled and laughed at his surprise. He handed the case to Lisa and watched as she turned and entered the tent.

Would his wife have liked Lisa? The American woman was unlike most of the women he knew, who all seemed born with a sense of style and sophistication—like Nura.

Lisa, on the other hand, had a freshness that was appealing. And an enthusiasm that had him captivated. He'd been hasty last night in accusing her of a conspiracy with his mother with the end result of marriage. If he'd thought it through, he'd have realized his mother would want him to marry a nice woman from Moquansaid, not someone from halfway around the world.

And in all fairness to Lisa, she had never actually flirted with him, never given him any real reason to suspect she was in league to interest him in a relationship.

He turned and started back to the helicopter. He'd keep in touch with the site via the radio in future. Make sure Lisa needed no further medical attention.

Professor Sanders hurried across the compound, obviously eager to speak with Tuareg.

"Sheikh al Shaldor, I did not recognize you when you were here before. We are most delighted to have you visit again. Is there anything I can show you or explain about the project?" he said when he caught up with Tuareg.

Tuareg greeted the professor. "You gave me an excellent tour last time. You are accomplishing more than expected. My uncle is pleased."

"It's so fascinating. I'd be happy if you'd care to stay

longer and have firsthand experience at the next layer we are uncovering. We fear we will lose important data if we don't move rapidly. There is the risk of damaging new discoveries, but time is so short. Unless we can have it extended?" he asked hopefully.

"That is not my area," Tuareg said. The dig was already costing his dam project time and money. He would as soon have the archeologists leave tomorrow so the long awaited reservoir could begin filling.

"Perhaps you might speak to your uncle on our behalf?" the professor asked tentatively.

"No. I am anxious to have the excavation completed. I am involved in the building of the dam."

"Ah, I see. Perhaps if you'd stay and visit longer. See what we are discovering, learn more about the people who lived here you would see how beneficial the excavation is?"

Tuareg had reached the helicopter. He had no intention of changing his mind. Still, he'd learned more than once never to close doors completely.

He glanced over toward Lisa's tent. Did he have time to come again?

The fact he wanted to surprised him.

"Perhaps. I will contact you if I decide to visit again." He'd see if he forgot the pretty photographer in the next couple of days. If not, maybe he'd return for a visit.

"We would love to have you stay for a day or two. Our accommodations won't be what you're used to, but I think you'll find the work so fascinating, you'll be able to overlook the inconveniences," the professor said.

"I am used to," Tuareg paused for just a second, "camping out."

So the door remained cracked open. With a word of farewell, Tuareg climbed into the helicopter and they were off.

Lisa sat on her cot. He was gone. She was used to good-byes. The first had been the cruelest—the death of her mother only a few feet away from her on a rainy night in Seattle. Then her father's death a couple of years later. The homes she'd lived in were like a kaleidoscope in her mind. The Brewsters the best. The Mahoneys the worst. Goodbye to Jill when she moved to California. Goodbye to—

She pulled herself up sharply. She was not giving in to some pity party. For a few days she'd known a fasci-nating man who'd stirred her senses and taken care of her in a time of need. She reached for her best camera and headed for the large tent. Time to catch up on what she missed while gone.

Wednesday was a blustery day. The sky was cloudy but without any immediate threat of rain. The wind blew in gusts and every time a particularly strong one came, Lisa looked up in remembrance. She was uneasy, as always when storms threatened. The tent billowed and flapped in the wind. She had papers anchored beneath several heavy rocks, a bowl, two cups and a camera.

The air gusted again and the tent shook. She looked around, afraid it would pull up its lines and sail away.

"Interesting way to hold down the paper," Tuareg said from the opening.

Lisa jumped in surprise and turned to look at him, startled to see him. He wore the traditional robes of the desert, a turban covering his dark hair, its end hanging free to leave his face clear. Her heart skipped a beat. She stared.

"I didn't know you were coming. I didn't hear the helicopter," she said, reaching out for one of the cups to anchor the page she was writing.

"There are other methods of travel in the desert," Tuareg said.

"You rode over?" she guessed.

"Ham needed the exercise. And the weather is threatening. I did not wish to fly in it."

She glanced around at the flimsy tent and prayed it would hold against whatever weather came.

"I did not expect to see you again," she said.

"Professor Sanders invited me. He hopes to get me to lobby my uncle to change his deadline for the expedition."

"That would be wonderful—if you would. There is so much here that is still not recovered. Think of the knowledge that will be lost once the water floods the site."

"Do not start. You know my views, I'm unlikely to change them," he said, walking around the tent, looking at the various articles on the long tables.

Lisa felt a flare of anger that he so arrogantly dismissed their arguments. She would not deny his project held great value, but not everything could be measured in monetary terms. "Knowledge is valuable for its own sake."

A gust of wind caused Tuareg's robes to billow, fluttering. "The weather seems to be growing worse."

"Then why are you here? Shouldn't you be home where it's safe and dry?"

"A little rain never hurt anyone."

Lisa looked away, remembering.

"I will talk with the professor and see more of the site he's so proud of. Then, perhaps after lunch, you may wish to accompany me to a camp nearby of nomads grazing sheep who will have to move before the flood waters rise."

Lisa was torn. She knew it was better not to spend time with Tuareg, but the enticing thought of actually being asked to spend an afternoon with him was more than she could resist.

"A short ride in a Jeep. A quick visit and we return," he said, coaxingly.

Put that way, how could she refuse? Actually, put any way, she wouldn't refuse.

After lunch, Tuareg wrapped the end of his scarf around his lower face so only his eyes were visible. He had received permission from Professor Sanders to drive one of the Jeeps. Urging Lisa to bring a scarf to protect her face against the blowing grit, he chose a Jeep and they were off. He spoke little once they were underway. There was no road or even track, just endless dirt, scrub brush and clumps of grass.

They soon reached the banks of the shallow river and turned to follow the languid flow. The vegetation was not as sparse near the water as it was just a few hundred yards away.

"All this will be lost when the water backs up, won't it?" she asked at one point, taken by a pretty setting of trees beside the river. The leafy abundance stood in stark contrast to the barren plains on which the excavation was taking place. There were a few date palms near the seep that gave water to the Wadi Hirum. Nothing like these thick green trees. The limbs moved in the gusting wind. The water danced with small ruffled waves.

"It will take a number of years for the reservoir to

reach its full capacity. But this will be one of the first areas to be flooded," he said, studying the landscape.

"Just think, these trees have been growing for more than a hundred years. We may be the last people on earth to see them," Lisa said, feeling a little sad.

"You are a romantic. It is the nature of things to grow, live, die. New trees will grow with the irrigation the reservoir will provide. Crops will flourish where now nothing grows."

"Hmm."

"Do you think progress should not be made?" he asked.

"Of course not. I'd hate to be living like my ancestors. But it's still too bad we can't find other ways to move forward and yet leave the beauty of nature as we find it."

"Take a picture."

"Great idea," she said, already reaching for her camera. She may be one of the last people to see these trees here, but a photograph would capture them forever.

She snapped a few frames, then looked at Tuareg. "How about you go over there and stand by the trees to give perspective to their size."

He didn't move for a moment, then nodded and climbed down from the Jeep. The sunshine sparkled off the river, the shade looked cool and inviting. An Arab prince in full robes lent a mysticism to the scene. Lisa happily snapped several shots. Only she would know who was in the photographs. The way he wore his robes and the cloth across his face hid all traces of who he was, adding to the magical aspect.

"Enough," he said a moment later and strode back to her side.

"Thank you. I'll send you copies if you like."

"No need. There are none I share photos with."

Lisa reseated her hat, resting her camera on her lap. She refused to feel sorry for Tuareg in light of his statement. He had his parents and other family members. Friends, undoubtedly. She had no family, but had a few close friends to share things with.

Unlike him, she was not cutting herself off from life.

The thought surprised her. And it wasn't true. He was not cutting himself off from life. The man was involved in a long-term project to better his country. He obviously was on good terms with his mother and, she suspected, his father. And well loved by many if the greetings at the party were anything to go by.

Yet there was a solitary air about him.

"We'll be at the settlement soon," he said.

Lisa would be glad to arrive. The jouncing of the Jeep was uncomfortable. And twice her foot had hit the floor hard, aggravating her ankle. Every time the Jeep seemed to lean sharply to the right, she felt fear. The car her mother had been driving that fateful night had rolled to the right before coming to rest on its roof. The memory seemed to be burned into her. She would never forget.

She looked eagerly ahead to see the tents when they began to materialize. The nomads had dwellings that could be quickly taken down and moved to another site of forage for their animals. The sheep munched vegetation near the river, strung out along the banks for as far as Lisa could see.

Tuareg stopped near a tent on the edge of the cluster of dun-colored structures. Before she knew it, Lisa had been introduced and given a cup of cool water. The inhabitants were reserved but friendly, greeting her formally. Tuareg translated the welcomes.

Before long, however, she had the women smiling and the few children jumping up and down with excitement. Especially when she brought out some butterscotch candies.

"They don't often get treats like that," Tuareg said. "It was nice of you to think of them."

"Hard candy is the only thing that seems to travel well in this heat. I'd love some dark chocolate myself. And Professor Sanders would give half a month's pay for some ice cream. I'm happy the children like the candy."

After some discussion, not at all pleasing to the men of the group, Tuareg suggested they walk around so Lisa could see the current camp of the nomads. The children danced around them as they walked, shyly smiling at Lisa and holding out their hands for more candy.

A couple of the older men accompanied them, talking with Tuareg. "They are not happy about the dam," Tuareg said softly at one point.

"Would you be if it changed your way of life?" Lisa asked. "It appears not everyone is as excited about this project as you. Certainly the archeologists aren't. Now these shepherds."

He shook his head. "Maybe not. But this will improve things."

"Change is hard to deal with—no matter if it is good for you," she said, stopping to gesture with her camera to the men with them. Tuareg said something to them in Arabic and they nodded, wide smiles breaking out. At least they seemed agreeable to having their photographs taken.

The afternoon sped by. When Tuareg said they had

to leave to reach the camp before dark, Lisa was reluctant to go.

The wind had died sometime during their visit. Everything was still, as if waiting. The land was old and had waited for centuries—just for Tuareg and his project? Would she return some day to see the desert blooming?

"Thank you for bringing me here. It's been fun seeing the children. I'm not around kids much."

"You should be. You seem to relate to them in a special way—even without a common language."

"You were there to translate."

They reached the expedition camp before dark. Dinner had already been started in the mess tent and Tuareg and Lisa quickly went to wash before joining the others.

He took off the robes and slung them over one of the stools near the row of sinks. Beneath he was wearing western attire. Lisa washed her face and hands and tried to stop the sexual awareness that spiked every time she was near the man. He was so off-limits for her. Remember that, Lisa! she admonished herself.

Professor Sanders was sitting in the mess tent at one table with two of the students who were working on the camp. He waved at Tuareg when he entered. In only moments Tuareg had sat at the professor's table and the two of them were deep in discussion.

Lisa hesitated, then deliberately sat at a table with some of the graduate students. As soon as she finished eating, she rose and left for her tent. She wanted to develop the photographs she'd taken that afternoon.

Some time later, caught up in rediscovering the scenes of the afternoon in the photos, she heard Tuareg call her. Lisa loved her quiet time. Now she knew she'd gladly give it up for more time with Tuareg.

"I'm here. Wait a moment, I'm at a critical juncture and don't want to ruin anything," she called, hoping he wouldn't open the black cloth.

Five minutes later, she pushed aside the dark cloth and entered the central part of her small tent. Tuareg sat on her cot, leafing through the pages of the pictures of Jeppa's party.

"I was hoping you'd take that to her. I'm not sure how to mail them," she said.

"These are excellent pictures. You didn't just take a snapshot, you've captured the essence of each person," he said. "There are two books."

"The second is for your mother, as a thank you for her kindness in inviting me to stay with her."

She glanced at her watch. It was after eleven. "Aren't you leaving?"

"The professor asked me to stay another day. He wants to see you," he said, shifting slightly to get more comfortable on her cot.

"Okay. Did you wish to see the pictures from today? I've developed the film and made a set of prints."

"Yes." He rose, towering above Lisa. His head brushed the top of her tent. She pushed through the makeshift dark room curtains. When he followed, she could feel the warmth from his skin they stood so close. The space was ample for one, not two.

The red light bathed everything in an eerie color. The pictures looked gray in the light, but the colors would be vibrant, she knew. She waited as Tuareg studied the pictures, hoping he'd like them.

"They're good. You've captured the feel for the

setting. I like that one of the little girl. Are you planning these for your book of Moquansaid?"

"Yes. These would be in the desert section. I still want pictures of the capital city to show the contrast."

He turned, brushing against Lisa's shoulder. She almost jumped. Her heart rate sped up. For one second she wished he'd kiss her. She almost leaned toward him. Appalled at her thoughts, she stepped back, bumping the table with the chemicals. He would be horrified if he knew how her mind worked. It would give more credence to the idea of his mother's matchmaking.

"I think I'll go see what the professor wants me for," she said. "Thank you again for taking me today."

Tuareg had merely been kind to a visitor to his country. Nothing more should be read into anything he had done.

"You wanted to see me, professor?" Lisa asked when she entered the big work tent where the artifacts were housed.

"Ah, yes." He looked over her shoulder, then beckoned her closer. "Do you realize who exactly Tuareg is?"

"The man who rescued me from the sandstorm," she said.

"He's also a man of influence with the man who granted our excavation rights. I thought if Tuareg could stay a few days, really see how important our discoveries are, maybe he'd convince his uncle to let us remain."

"We're scheduled to leave at the end of August." Only nine weeks away.

"I know, but I can get an extension on my leave from the university. Most of us would be able to remain until the weather proved to be too inclement to work. Talk to Tuareg, convince him to use his influence with his uncle."

"I can't do that, even if I thought it would work. I don't have that kind of relationship with him. He's merely been kind to someone who he found during a sandstorm."

"Nonsense. You are a pretty girl, Lisa. I hardly need tell a woman how to use her wiles to get her way," the professor said.

Lisa laughed. "I think you've been buried in the past too long. Anyway, I'm hardly his type. I regret the deadline as much as anyone here. But I am not going to exert undue influence on Tuareg or any member of his family on our behalf. We knew when we arrived what the terms were."

"But if they could be changed!"

"Then it has to be done without my input."

She turned and walked back outside, almost crashing into Tuareg. It would be too much to hope he hadn't heard.

She smiled nervously, aware with every inch of her body just how close they stood. Stepping around him, she began walking away from the tent.

"The professor suggested you may wish to stay longer," she said. "To see how they are progressing on the dig. He—actually we all—very much wish we could stay beyond the original deadline."

"I heard."

"Oh."

He stopped her and swung her around to face him. It was dark in the compound, only faint light showing from the tents. She could hardly make out Tuareg's features.

"I would not change the deadline except to move it up. When the agreed time arrives, the professor and his team departs."

"I know." She sighed.

"Lisa, you are a woman of honor."

She blinked. What could she say to something like that. "Thank you."

He laughed softly. "You sound annoyed. Women prefer to be told they are beautiful. That they smell as sweet as the most fragrant flower. Their eyes rival the stars. Their lips are more delectable than the plumpest pomegranates."

She tilted her face and gazed up at the stars. They were sharp and clear in the desert night. If she didn't look at him, didn't listen closely to the mocking tones, she could almost pretend he were wooing her, caressing her with words. Painting a picture that would stay with her forever.

"It's so beautiful here. I love it," she said softly.

He leaned over and brushed his lips against hers.

She blinked and stepped back, startled.

He watched her carefully, then gently drew her away from the main path and into the shadows. Enfolding her into his arms, he pulled her close and kissed her again. This was no mere brush of lips but the powerful kiss of a determined man. After a second's hesitation, she returned the kiss, moving her mouth against his, opening for him when he teased. Heat seemed to spread from the soles of her feet to the top of her head. Breathing became difficult, but not needed. She had all she'd ever want in life with this kiss.

When he ended it, Lisa almost groaned in disappointment.

He took her hand. "Come, walk with me. We can look at the stars and feel the heartbeat of the desert."

He led the way, heading opposite to the dig site so at least she didn't have to worry about falling into any trenches. She wondered if he could see better in the dark than she could. The stars were bright, but there was no full moon to illuminate their way.

The silence grew as they left the soft murmur of voices behind. Soon only the soft sound of the breeze among the grass and caressing her skin could be heard.

"You have a strong affinity for the desert," she said.

"My people have lived on this land for centuries. It's a part of me. I could live my entire life here and not miss the city at all."

That confirmed what Lisa expected. While Tuareg was polished and sophisticated in the city surroundings she'd seen him in, he seemed much more connected to the untamed land of the desert.

Tuareg wanted to ask Lisa how she liked the desert. It did not call to all. The nomads who made it home, the people who had carved a country out of barren land—for them and their descendants a special bond had been forged. Never to be severed. But Lisa didn't come from such a background.

He stopped and, in a second, she stopped as well. They were alone. The sound of the night was elusive, there only for those who would listen.

Why had he kissed her? He'd dated once or twice since Nura's death. The events had been meaningless. He was better off spending time by himself or with family.

Yet something about this woman intrigued him. Had him temporarily neglecting duty to spend time with her.

Her lips had been as delectable as they'd looked. Her eyes fascinated him. She fascinated him.

He frowned, not liking the fact. He had no business thinking of another woman.

Yet Nura was gone. Had been for years. She was never coming back.

Tuareg wanted to capture the love he'd had for his wife. She'd been special. But time lent perspective. Nura had been his first love. His only love. He'd been faithful to her since they'd been children. She was special. But she had not been perfect.

He could remember the fights they'd had. Usually over something minor yet with all the passion each possessed. Days passed when she wouldn't speak to him. Maybe he'd not liked her as much as he normally did on those days. But he'd always loved her.

And on one point they had never agreed. She'd known he wanted children, but had refused until they'd had enough fun to last her a lifetime. He'd thought having children would also be fun. Seeing the ones today reminded him of the happy hours he and his parents had shared when he and his siblings had been younger.

He was drawn to Lisa Sullinger and didn't want to be. He'd rather live his life on his own terms. She would be returning to the United States at the end of the summer. Their worlds were too divergent to ever mix. He could give himself all the reasons in the world.

Yet there was something about her that fascinated him. She was always enthusiastic. Was that it? Or was it her delight in every aspect of life no matter how mundane? Or perhaps her optimism? Her way of seeing things with rose-colored glasses where most people would rail against fate? She had had a sad life losing her parents so young. Yet he'd never met a person with a sunnier outlook on life.

She reached out and touched his arm. He felt a tingle of awareness that had been missing from his life.

Frowning, he glanced at her, resisting. He didn't want any entanglements.

"I think we should go back now. It's getting late and you need to find out where you're bunking."

He lifted his eyes to the stars. Their brilliance rivaled any glittering lights man made. The desert spoke, cooling down after the heat of the day. He should leave. There was no reason to stay.

"The professor suggested I share his tent," Tuareg said. "Do you suppose it was to lobby for extension of the deadline?"

Lisa shook her head. "More likely it is the best one in camp and he's aware you are a sheikh. Be warned, it won't be like yours."

He turned and walked beside her back to the cluster of tents to the one the professor used. He'd leave in the morning. After he saw Lisa again.

CHAPTER SEVEN

LISA KEPT TO HERSELF the next morning. She couldn't believe Tuareg had kissed her or that she'd kissed him back. It had taken her forever to fall asleep last night. She'd relived that magical moment a hundred times. And fantasized a million different scenarios in which he'd kiss her again.

She left her tent a little later than usual. Breakfast was buffet style, so she could still get something to eat before beginning work. She was surprised to see the horse dozing in the makeshift corral. She thought Tuareg would have left at sunrise.

Rounding the corner by the mess tent, she came upon Tuareg and Professor Sanders standing in the shade. The professor held something in his hand and he and Tuareg were studying it.

Lisa stopped abruptly. Tuareg caught the movement and raised his gaze. She could read nothing from his eyes. Did he regret last night?

Professor Sanders turned and smiled. "Ah, Lisa. Just the person. Here's another porcelain statue, this of a small animal. Do you think it is a tiger? Maybe traded from the caravan, I was thinking." He held out the small object.

Automatically she raised her camera and took a picture.

Tuareg watched. "Maybe the professor wanted you to take it and look at it, not film it," he said.

She lowered the camera and looked at him.

"You seem to live life through the lens of a camera, rather than facing it head on," he commented.

Struck by the idea, Lisa hesitated a moment. She slung the camera strap over her shoulder and reached for the small statue. It was warm to the touch. Dirt clung to the crevices. She looked at it, but Tuareg's words echoed. Did he really think she didn't embrace life? Wasn't she here on this adventure instead of opting for a safe and boring routine in Seattle?

"Beautiful, isn't it?" the professor said, gazing at it.

"It is lovely," Lisa said. Her imagination sparked an image of a woman long ago who had been given this by a lover. How she must have treasured something so valuable and fragile—all the more so because of the giver.

She raised her eyes and met Tuareg's dark gaze. For a moment she could imagine he'd given her something as precious. If he ever did, she would treasure it and keep it with her wherever she went.

Gently she laid it back in the professor's hand. "No idea where it came from?" she asked. "I mean, from China or India? Would it have been a gift or a payment for something?"

"That we may never know. But this makes two fine statues, existing in an area of the world where porcelain was not common. Obviously brought by caravan. Don't you think they found these beautiful beyond anything they'd ever seen?"

"Judging from the stone carvings you've discovered, these were far finer than anything this group was capable of. Whoever owned them was probably considered the wealthiest member of the group," Tuareg said.

Lisa continued to the mess tent. She didn't like Tuareg's comment about her hiding behind her camera. Her friend Bailey said that sometimes. Lisa argued with her, but now another had said it. Could it be true?

She was slow to make friends, but that was because she feared making connections and then losing them. She'd become attached to her first foster mother after only a few weeks and had been heartbroken when she'd been moved from that home to another. She'd learned over the years to be careful where she bestowed her affections. It was safer to remain a bit aloof and not risk hurting her heart again.

But she didn't hide from life.

It was hot in the tent. She picked up her food and went outside to eat. The faint stirring of air kept it cooler than the enclosed tent. She found a spot in the shade from the overhang of the mess tent and sat down. Eating the croissant, she tried to imagine what the village they were excavating would have looked like five hundred years ago. The small trees were dependent on the subsurface water of the Wadi. Only during the rainy season was there plentiful water. The river was nearby.

The structures most likely would have been the color of the baked desert dirt. They would have been simple structures for shelter. Children would have played in front of the homes. Men would have tended the sheep or tried to grow something to eat. Women would have done the cooking. What had the house where the statues were found have been like?

She could imagine the men looking a lot like Tuareg, strong and fearless. Capable of dealing with the harshness of the land. He'd have fit in five hundred years ago as easily as he did today.

She heard footsteps and looked up. Tuareg walked toward her. He drew near and sank on the sand next to her. "I planned to leave first thing this morning, but your professor talked me into staying longer," he said.

He gazed around at the landscape. "A lonely place to live all those centuries ago, wouldn't you think?" he asked.

"They had family, friends. It was their way of life. They knew no other. I bet they were thrilled with the caravans that passed. Imagine what they dreamed of when speaking to the men leading camels laden with fantastic goods."

Tuareg laughed. Lisa blinked. It was the first time she'd heard him laugh.

"What's funny?"

"Your romanticized version. They were probably hardheaded tradesmen milking the caravans for as much booty as they could get away with. They most likely bargained for water in the dry season, sold grazing rights for grass for the camels."

"I like my version better," she murmured, feeling suddenly tongue-tied, unable to forget their kiss last night. Wishing with all her heart that he'd kiss her again.

"I'm leaving soon. I'll take one more look at the trench, then get Ham back home."

He rose and held out a hand to help her rise. She took it, letting go as soon as she was on her feet.

She swallowed hard and tried not to let the disappointment show. What had she expected, that he'd immediately say he wanted to stay, to spend time with her? Or sweep her into his arms and kiss her again?

He looked at her, his eyes dark and mysterious. She felt her heart flutter. His wife had been a lucky woman.

He reached out and rested his hands on her shoulders, drawing her closer. Kissing her a second later.

Lisa closed her eyes, the bright sunshine temporarily hidden as she savored the feel of his lips against hers, the teasing of his tongue, the fulfillment of his kiss. Sensuous yearning filled her. She wanted to be closer, to feel his body against hers, to have him sweep her away somewhere special just for the two of them.

She pulled back. It was broad daylight and they were at the side of the mess tent. Anyone could walk by. She wasn't sure what the kiss was about, was it merely farewell? Or something more.

"Lisa—"

"No, don't say anything. I think it's time to say goodbye. Thank you for all you've done for me. I appreciate it. But you yourself said this would go nowhere."

She turned and almost ran into the mess tent, dumping her plate and cup in the bin and catching her breath. She stood still, trying to hear Tuareg walk away.

"Do you need anything?" the student who had been designated dishwasher for this morning asked.

"No. Just, um, thinking." She turned and slowly went back to the large opening. Stepping outside she was relieved to see Tuareg gone. A moment later she heard the horse, but she kept her eyes down as she made her way to the work tent.

This archeological site would vanish before long, only her pictures would remain to show what once had been.

She might be destined to stay alone her whole life, but she could still leave something important behind.

Tuareg urged Ham away from the site and toward his tent. He hadn't meant to kiss Lisa again. He was not a man to give misleading gestures. Any woman would be justified to think he was interested by the attention he'd paid over the last couple of days—especially kissing her.

And he was not. He'd had his one chance at love and it had ended abruptly.

He needed to get back to his normal routine and not let Lisa distract him. She had almost run from that kiss. She was wiser than he.

Yet there were regrets. He'd enjoyed sharing the desert with someone who seemed to like it as much as he did. Nura never had. Tuareg waited expectantly. But the searing pain didn't come. Just warmth and gentle memories of the woman he'd loved. Was he healing? Was the tearing grief from the early days finally easing?

He looked around the landscape he loved. There were no memories of Nura here. She had never gone with him when he'd sought the calming influence by staying a few nights. Watching Lisa, he knew she felt totally differently about the land. According to Professor Sanders, Lisa often took off, as she had the day he met her, to explore, liking the solitude and the unexpected sights she found.

Yesterday she'd delighted in photographing the empty landscape as much as the children. Nothing as far as the eye could see but the clumps of grasses that had prevailed against the arid land and the few trees along the river, yet she'd found these worthwhile to capture on film.

Lisa was totally different from any woman he knew. She interested him with her openness and friendly demeanor. And enticed him with her smile and laughter. His life had been devoid of laughter for a long time.

Was that reason enough to want a woman? Or was there more? He'd like to take her away somewhere for a few days, learn more about her life, her dreams. Hear that laugher sparkle in the night. Awaken to her blue-gray eyes smiling into his.

Tuareg turned away from the image. It was impossible. But the longing didn't abate. Maybe he'd never love another, but he wanted Lisa.

And for the first time he didn't feel guilty about his desire. He was alive. Nura loved life, she would not have wanted him to shut himself away from the joys of living. She wrung every precious moment from her existence. Could he do less? To do so would dishonor what she valued.

Tuareg spurred his horse on and rode like the wind. He couldn't outrun the images in his mind, but he could try. He had only to reach the tent. Another day of solitude and he'd return to the capital city and plunge into the tasks that awaited. Work would bring forgetfulness.

After lunch, Professor Sanders asked that everyone join him in the work tent to pack the artifacts. What had been uncovered was being shipped to the state museum in Soluddai.

Lisa was assigned the task of keeping track of each item being packed in each crate and then pasting one copy of the inventory on the outside of each box.

"Tuareg arranged for this to be picked up and delivered this week. And for periodic pickups between now and the end of August," the professor said.

The camaraderie among the archeologists, both students and professors, was well established. Sometimes Lisa felt as if they talked in code. Once again she was on the outside looking in. Part of the group, yet not one with it.

As she worked, she wished Tuareg would come and

take her for a ride on his horse along the banks of the river. She shifted on the stool, thinking that she should wish her ankle miraculously healed so she could walk to the river by herself. Not that she could swim in that water, but it was always cooler in the shade of the old trees.

By the time dinner was ready, all the artifacts had been labeled and packed and the boxes were stacked near the tent. Tuareg had agreed to send transportation from Soluddai in the morning. Professor Sanders would accompany the cartons and turn them over to the minister of antiquities. One set of inventory lists and photographs would stay with the boxes, two copies would remain in camp for reference and one set was already packaged for mailing back to the university in Washington.

Lisa arose early the next morning. She heard unusual activity in the camp and after dressing went to the food tent. Several of the archeologists were eating, others had already been and gone.

"We're getting earlier starts now under professor's orders," one of the students said when Lisa asked why so much activity so early. "He wants every hour possible spent on the dig."

"When do the trucks arrive?" one of the women asked.

"After ten," someone called.

"Good, that'll give the professor a few hours of work before taking off for Soluddai," she said. "He'll spend every moment in the trench, I expect." With a friendly wave, she took her tray to the washing area and left.

Lisa got a cup of coffee and sat at one table with some fruit and cheese. She didn't have much to do until new items were unearthed. When she finished eating she'd go to the excavation to see where they were working today and if they needed photos of the site. If not, was her ankle up to driving a Jeep and taking another foray into the desert?

When she drew near the trench a short time later, she saw the flurry of activity. Everyone seemed to be at one end of the wide excavation.

Knowing something was up, Lisa quickened her pace.

"What's going on?" Lisa asked when she reached the group.

"We've found a burial site," one of the women said with excitement.

"Paul found it when he started a new direction," another said.

"Bones and some artifacts. More than one, it looks like," yet another said.

"This is amazing," someone else said in a hushed tone.

Lisa felt the excitement of the group. Would this be enough of a find to extend their deadline? She hoped so, but there was no telling how Tuareg's uncle would view this latest discovery. Tuareg wanted the dam to begin functioning this fall, to bring water to this area. A delay might mean another year before the reservoir would begin filling.

She peered over the edge, mesmerized by the careful work the archeologists were doing to uncover the bones.

When the two large trucks arrived promptly at ten, Lisa had returned to the work tent. Since almost all the artifacts were being shipped, she gave directions to the drivers on which few cartons remained. Where was the professor?

The trucks were almost loaded when Lisa saw him hurrying toward the compound.

"Lisa, thank goodness. There will have to be a

change in plans. I cannot leave the site in light of what we discovered this morning," he said when he reached her. "I'm needed here. We all are. I don't know if the sheikh will extend our deadline because of this discovery. In case he refuses, we need to get as much revealed as we can. I cannot afford time away from the site. You'll have to go in my stead."

"Me? I can't talk with the minister of antiquities. He's expecting an archeologist, not a photographer."

"You're a member of this team. You'll have to do it. Quickly, run and pack what you'll need. You have the notebooks and pictures. Write down any questions you cannot answer and I'll work on them upon your return. This discovery is too important to leave."

Lisa didn't hesitate. She wasn't needed here, but the professor was. She hastened to her tent to pack for two days in the capital city. In only a few moments she was back, bag and camera case in hand.

"Professor, who will take pictures of the discovery?" she asked.

"Oh, I hadn't thought about that. Maybe one of the students. Which camera should they use?"

It took almost a half hour for Lisa to instruct the student designated as temporary photographer. She left plenty of film with instructions not to attempt to develop the rolls, she would do so when she returned.

Finally, she climbed into the front of the lead truck and settled in. It was hot even with the windows open. She hoped the vehicle had air conditioning.

The professor gave her some last-minute instructions. "Tuareg was to meet me at the museum. Ask him to handle anything you can't," the professor said as the driver slammed shut his door and started the engine.

Lisa hadn't known Tuareg would be there. She had thought they'd said goodbye. Apparently not a final farewell.

The drive to the capital was uncomfortable. The large trucks lurched and bounced on the rough road. She hoped everything had been packed securely enough to survive intact. She briefly thought of taking pictures on the ride, but she never would have gotten a clear shot.

Thankfully, while still many miles from the city they reached paved roads and the ride became smoother.

Lisa was glad when the driver called to say they would reach the museum in only another half hour. Her anticipation at seeing Tuareg rose with each passing mile.

CHAPTER EIGHT

LISA HAD BEEN RESOLUTE in saying goodbye to Tuareg. Now it seemed as if the fates had stepped in to grant her a few more hours of his company. She watched eagerly as the driver navigated the city streets. She recognized the huge terra-cotta building when they turned onto the main avenue. Her heart thrilled at the sight.

When they reached the museum, there were several men in suits awaiting them out front. One had a clipboard and stepped up to the first truck that parked. He would remain to check off the boxes as the truck drivers unloaded them.

Tuareg was also waiting there. His expression of surprise let Lisa know he hadn't expected her. Was there disapproval in his face as well?

Introductions were made when she climbed down from the high cab of the truck.

"Where is Professor Sanders?" Tuareg asked.

Lisa stepped closer, her emotions mixed at seeing him again. This was strictly business. But she still felt her heart flutter the way it always did around him. "He was unable to attend. He sent me in his place."

The man next to Tuareg glanced at her and dismissed

her without a word. His attention turned to Tuareg. "We were expecting the professor. I wished to review the artifacts with him and go over his timetable for completion before the deadline imposed by His Excellency."

Tuareg glanced at Lisa. "Apparently you must deal with Miss Sullinger. She is the official representative of the expedition. I merely arranged transportation. Lisa, this is Mohammad bin Algariq, minister of antiquities."

The man drew a sharp breath. Lisa almost smiled at the expression of resignation on his face. Slowly he turned to study her.

"Very well. If you will come with me." He walked away without another word.

"Friendly, isn't he?" she murmured. With a glance at Tuareg, she dutifully followed the minister. Tuareg fell into step beside her. "I'll serve as translator," he murmured.

She nodded, then hurried to keep up with Mr. bin Algariq. It wouldn't do to become lost in the vast museum.

The next two hours were uncomfortable. Lisa knew the director disliked dealing with her, he made that abundantly clear. There were plenty of questions posed for which she did not know the answer. She carefully jotted them in a notebook. He grew more impatient with each unanswered query, but she only had the hastily given information from the professor and did her best to hold her own.

Once or twice Tuareg said something in Arabic to the man. It seemed to placate him for a few moments, but then his frustration rose again.

She was tired by the time the minister walked them back to the entrance.

A limo sat in the same spot where the trucks had been. Tuareg gently guided her toward the vehicle.

"You survived," he said.

"Barely. I'm not the lofty leader of the expedition, merely a flunky. I think the director was miffed someone of more importance wasn't sent."

"He'll get over it. I know he's delighted with the objects found at the dig," Tuareg said. The chauffeur had the back door opened and ushered them into the cool interior of the limo.

Settling back, Lisa felt rejuvenated just being in Tuareg's presence.

"Thank you for arranging for all the artifacts to be brought here before the end of the summer. He was impressed by the figurines, wasn't he? I know the professor will be pleased to have the invitation to stop by before departing."

She looked out the window. "Where are we going?" The professor hadn't even told her about the return trip. She was to remain in the capital for a couple of days on call for the museum in case other questions arose. Had he booked a room at a hotel nearby?

"We had a room at a hotel reserved for Professor Sanders. You, however, would be welcome to stay at my mother's apartment if you wish. Unfortunately, she flew to Paris a couple of days ago to join my father. But the staff remains. She would be most delighted to know you stayed there."

"I couldn't impose. The hotel will be fine."

"I think my mother's apartment would be better." His tone suggested arguing would be futile.

"Very well, then. Thank you." It would be nice to return to the lovely apartment.

"Perhaps you would join me for dinner," Tuareg said. Another few hours together.

"I would very much enjoy that," she said. She looked out the window as the buildings swept by. She was too tired to think about photography now, but maybe in the morning she could take a walk and get some pictures. Not too far a walk though; her ankle was still not one hundred percent.

"Where would you like to go for dinner?" Tuareg asked.

She knew nothing about restaurants in Soluddai. And she really didn't feel like going someplace where everyone would be dressed up except her.

"You know what I'd love? An American hamburger with all the fixings." She looked at him wondering what his reaction might be. "Do you have places that sell food like that?"

"And what are the fixings?"

"French fries, onion rings and a bun piled high with lettuce, tomato and mustard and mayo."

He frowned. "Does all that taste good together?"

"Have you never had a hamburger with all the fixings?" she asked in mock dismay. "I thought you were a worldly traveler."

Slowly Tuareg shook his head, his eyes watching her.

Lisa laughed. "I'm teasing. If you find us a store, I'll buy everything and make you the best hamburger you'll ever have. That is if we can use your mother's kitchen."

"You'd cook it yourself?" he asked.

"Sure, why not? Wait, don't tell me you don't cook for yourself."

"Why would I when I employ several fine cooks?"

"Didn't your wife cook and you help out?"

"No," he replied. "Maybe she cooked as a girl but she had no need once we were married."

"Oh." She gave it a bit of thought, then shook away all doubts. She'd love to have a hamburger. And maybe show Tuareg the fun of cooking together.

"Then you can be my apprentice and we'll fix it together."

"That should prove interesting," he murmured.

Tuareg was amused by the enthusiasm Lisa showed for preparing a meal. She asked to be taken to a market that carried western food. His chauffeur found one on a street near the American and British embassies. Soon Tuareg and Lisa were walking up and down aisles of packaged food. Had he ever been in a supermarket before? He didn't think so.

Lisa pushed a cart and stopped now and then to place articles in it. Mustard came in yellow plastic bottles. Ketchup came in clear bottles showing the red sauce. Chopped pickles in another jar. Soon there were more items than he'd expect to need for a relatively simple meal. He knew what hamburgers were. He just wasn't sure they were the delicacy Lisa seemed to think they were.

Once they reached his mother's apartment, he directed the chauffeur to carry the sacks of supplies to the kitchen and inform the kitchen staff they were dismissed for the night. He almost shared the astonishment the man displayed.

"You'll have the bedroom you had before. Would you like to shower first?" he asked.

"Yes, thank you. I'll hurry. Shall we meet in the kitchen at six?"

Tuareg watched her walk away, wondering what he was in store for. Nura had never cooked anything as far as he knew. Nor did his mother or aunt. Was cooking an art left to only the working class?

He went to a second guest room to clean up—already anticipating the cooking adventure with Lisa.

Lisa ran the water hot and stood beneath it for a long time. When she finally had enough, she was delighted to find the dress she'd hung out had lost most of the travel wrinkles. She put it on, dried her hair and wandered back to the main rooms of the apartment.

She heard Tuareg and turned, her heart catching when she saw him.

"Time to cook?" he asked whimsically.

"Just about. I don't know where the kitchen is, though," she said.

He led the way.

The kitchen was a cook's dream. The gas stove had six burners and a grill. The stainless steel refrigerator was industrial size. The counters were granite, the butcher-block table in the center was huge. She quickly saw her dry ingredients on the counter neatly stacked. The rest was probably in the refrigerator.

"Okay, let's get started."

Lisa rummaged around for a moment, finding knives, bowls, pans and other items she wanted.

Taking the potatoes, she beckoned Tuareg.

"First we wash them to get the dirt off, then we'll cut them into thick strips for french fries."

She showed him how to do it. Once he was working, she pulled out the other items she wanted.

Lisa glanced over and bit back a smile. The setting was quite domestic. And probably something Tuareg never expected to do. She'd never thought much about it before, but if she ever married, she'd love to spend the end of the day together with her husband, preparing their evening meal. They'd talk about their day, make plans for the future.

"Is this something you do often?" he asked. A nice pile of sliced potatoes cut with precision was growing.

"Have friends over to cook dinner? Yes. Or I go to their places. We barbecue a lot in nice weather—which isn't often, I can tell you. Seattle has a rainy climate and is too cold in winter."

Lisa told him about her friends Bailey and Sara and how they experimented with a wide variety of cuisines when younger.

Once finished with his task, Tuareg brought over the potatoes and put them where Lisa indicated. He then went and settled on one of the high stools. He watched Lisa continue to bustle around. She thought about assigning him something else to do, but could do everything faster herself. She was glad he continued to stay with her, however.

He asked for more details on why the professor had not come. She told him about the burial site and the excitement it had caused.

When she fell silent, she glanced around, once again aware of how different their lives were. He'd never cooked, shopped for food or had a barbecue with friends. How strange that seemed to her. Did he think her lifestyle equally strange?

"You've grown pensive," he said.

"I was just thinking how different your life is from mine. I don't know a single person who has a cook, much less more than one. I guess it'd be fun to have meals prepared by someone else, except I do enjoy cooking."

"What else do you enjoy?" he asked.

She put the ground meat patties on a broiling pan and slid them into the oven. "Domestically I enjoy baking and working with the plants I have on my small patio. Bailey's watching them for me while I'm gone."

"You have an apartment, not a house?"

"I couldn't afford a house. My apartment is nothing like this one, however." Her one-bedroom place was small, with no view. But it was near the waterfront and she could walk to Pike Place Market in only a few minutes.

She drew out the pan and flipped the burgers.

"You said you have an apartment in the city?" she said.

"A pied-à-terre, really. I acquired it after Nura died. I don't stay in the city more than I need to for business."

"Because you prefer the desert."

"Exactly."

Tuareg bit into his hamburger some moments later with trepidation. The burgers were juicy and flavorful and he followed Lisa's example and piled the bun high with relish, tomato, lettuce and onion slices. She watched warily, hoping he'd think the meal worth the preparation.

"No wonder you were dreaming of something like this. It is delicious," he said.

She nodded, relieved he liked it. For a few moments she felt at home. Traveling was fun, but she longed for her own things, her friends. She felt lonely at the dig where all the archeologists had more in common with each other than with her.

When she reached for the iced water they were drinking she said, "I told you this was terrific food. We haven't had anything like this at the site. Not a bad trade-off for the special work being done there, but absence makes it all the more appealing when I do get it."

"As with the shower," he said.

"Right. Or the ice cream the professor misses. Anyway, I appreciate your letting me cook tonight."

When they finished eating, Lisa sipped her water and looked around the kitchen. "It won't take long to clean up," she said.

"Leave it. Someone will clean it in the morning."

She shook her head. "That's not right. We made the mess, we need to clean it."

"I pay people to do that."

Hopping off the stool, she reached for his plate. "I still want to clean the dishes."

She was stubborn. He could order her to leave everything as it was, but he had a feeling she'd just ignore him and do as she wished. Not many people ignored his orders.

A half hour later the last pan was dried. Lisa nodded in satisfaction as she looked around the immaculate room.

"I believe this is the longest I've ever been in a kitchen," Tuareg said. "Can we leave now?" He had enjoyed himself this evening. For a moment he wondered if every meal would be as much fun if Lisa were around or was this a one-off deal. Surely she'd appreciate others cooking for her on a daily basis.

She nodded, a happy smile lighting her face. He didn't understand the appeal of cleaning, but had been intrigued watching her change of expression. Her eyes were a silvery gray tonight. What did that mean?

"In my circle of friends, the kitchen is the heart of the home. Everyone gathers there if we are getting together for a meal. Good friends, that is. If it's a big party, then another room is more suitable."

"I believe we are more formal." He never knew Nura to go into the kitchen except to instruct the cook on what to prepare for a special meal. Her friends liked to gather in the salon, or meet at clubs where the entertainment was more exciting than a quiet evening at home.

Surprisingly, he no longer wished to go out to such places. He was more than content to spend a quiet evening with Lisa talking, learning more about her. Trying to guess how she would react to things was entertainment enough. Though that was probably unfair to her. Maybe they could go out later or tomorrow night. The professor had planned to stay two days, wasn't Lisa going to be here as long?

Tuareg escorted Lisa into the salon. She went to the window, gazing out over the lights that had come on throughout the city. He remembered the other night when she'd been so delighted with the lights. And the end result.

He wasn't making assumptions tonight.

"I never get tired of sights like this," she said.

"Perhaps you'd like to go out, see some of the city at night? There are some clubs that offer excellent entertainment."

She turned and tilted her head slightly as she gazed at him. "I'd rather drive around and see how everything sparkles at night. I'm not up to dancing or anything with my ankle."

"I'll call for the limo."

"And I'll get my camera."

He hesitated by the doorway. "No, tonight is for you to enjoy, not be working."

"It's not work. Think how great night photos would

look in my book." She was quiet a moment, then wrinkled her nose again. "You're right, it is work. Okay, no camera."

Fifteen minutes later they were sitting side by side in the limo. Tuareg closed the window between them and the driver after giving him instructions to drive around the different sections of the city.

Lisa looked eagerly out the window as they drove.

"Tell me about Soluddai. Is it Moquansaid's oldest city?"

"Oldest one continually occupied." Tuareg wasn't sure he wanted to be a tour guide, yet what had he expected when offering the drive? He suspected he had thought more about getting away from the apartment and the temptation it offered than the actual drive.

Now he sat even closer to her than he would have at the salon. He could smell her fragrance, almost feel the silky touch of her hair.

Lisa was nervous, and when nervous, she talked more than she should. Every time Tuareg paused, she asked another question. She was aware of him like she'd never been aware of another man. She could have listened to him all night long. His deep voice sounded like dark wine might sound. And was almost as intoxicating.

The warmth from his body seemed to fill the back of the car. She never knew how much longing to lean against another person would be hard to resist. The sweet torture was driving her crazy, but she wouldn't want to be another place on earth!

The lights at street level were so bright that some areas looked almost like day. She couldn't read the Arabic script that flashed and glowed in neon, but ap-

preciated the variety of colors blending together in a
rainbow of hues, each brighter than the last.

"Where are we now?" she asked as they drove along
a busy thoroughfare.

"The primary tourist area. These restaurants and night-
clubs cater to Europeans and are open far into the night."

Lisa glanced at him. "Is this where you used to come
with your wife? You said she liked to entertain away
from home."

"Sometimes."

Lisa noted he rarely talked about his wife. She
guessed the hurt of her death was still too strong. She
had heard often enough how devoted they'd been to
each other.

It was late when they returned to the apartment.
Tuareg escorted her to the front door and bid her good
night there.

Lisa went straight to bed. Two hours later she awoke
with a start. A storm had blown in. She hadn't noticed
any signs on their drive, but then she'd been focused on
the sights, not the clouds in the sky.

Lightning illuminated the sky. Thunder cracked immediately. She shivered, huddling beneath the covers.
Rain poured down in rivulets on the windows. Lisa had
left the curtains opened to enjoy the ambiance of the
night lights. Now she could see the fury of the storm
without impediment.

She swallowed hard, all thought of sleep gone. Once
again she was a little girl caught in the smashed car
calling for her mother.

Shivering despite the warmth of the bed, she gazed
out the window, mesmerized by what she saw. She was
dry and safe. Yet the old fear crowded her throat and her

hands felt clammy. When she'd awoken with nightmares after her mother's death, her father had gathered her close, keeping her safe. After his death, there was no one.

Sometimes, she'd have given anything to have the comfort of another when she awoke remembering.

How long would the storm last? It seemed like forever. Yet a half hour later the worst had passed. She could still hear the faint rumble of thunder occasionally but the sky no longer lit up bright as day and the rain soon ceased.

She rose and put on another shirt over her nightshirt. Padding quietly to the kitchen, she prepared herself some warm milk. She needed something to calm her nerves if she was to get back to sleep. It was after four in the morning. She had not had enough sleep to remain awake. Yet her heart still pounded and the memories crowded in. She wished she knew Tuareg's phone number. She could have at least called him for someone to talk to.

The next morning, Maliq knocked on Lisa's door, pushing it open and entering carrying a tray of hot chocolate and warm croissants.

Lisa had slept past the time she'd planned to waken. She didn't recognize the maid at first, then was delighted to see a familiar face.

"I didn't know you worked here as well," she said.

"I do not. His Excellency had me brought here because I speak English and he said you'd be staying for a few days. It's my pleasure to be here. I have brought you breakfast," Maliq said. "His Excellency asks if you'd like to see some more of the city today."

"I'd love to. I've been wanting to take some pictures." Today she'd bring her camera.

Maliq set the tray on her lap. "I will let him know. The time given was ten. Plenty of time to get dressed after you eat." She bowed slightly and quietly left the room.

Lisa ate the buttery croissant and sipped the rich hot chocolate. Such luxury. A person could get very used to it.

Once she was full, she moved the tray and rose to dress. She checked her watch. It was almost ten. Being up several hours in the middle of the night played havoc with schedules.

Once dressed, she checked her camera case and was ready.

She headed for the salon. Tuareg was sitting on the sofa, portable phone at his ear. He noticed Lisa as soon as she stepped inside and rose. A moment later he tossed the phone onto a table and came to greet her.

"Camera at the ready?" he asked.

"I can't miss this opportunity. This book is important to me."

"So we're off. I thought after we finished our drive, we could have lunch at my home. It's a short drive from the city."

"Lovely." She'd like to see his place again. The gardens had been spectacular. This visit, she could actually walk around them.

When they reached the sidewalk, Lisa was surprised to find a small red sports car at the curb. The convertible top had been folded.

"Better to take pictures with," Tuareg said, ushering her into the front seat.

"Is this yours?"

"It is," he said, sliding behind the wheel.

"And do you drive very fast in it?"

"Most days. But not today. We'll go at a snail's pace so you can get your pictures."

She laughed, feeling carefree and happy. Another few stolen hours to enjoy with Tuareg.

Lisa leaned her head back, able to see everything without a roof. She brought out her camera and put it on her lap. She was ready.

Soluddai was a contrast of Arabic architecture and modern skyscrapers. Sometimes she felt as if she were in Los Angeles or Seattle. Others, in a time past. The ornate carvings and inlaid tiles gave a richness to the Arabic buildings that she captured with delight.

"I love the distinctive styles, so very different, yet blending together," she said, snapping a shot of a tall steel structure. "Sort of like the people I see on the side-walks. Some are in traditional attire, others in clothes worn in Paris and Rome."

"Soluddai is a cosmopolitan city," he murmured, driving easily through the heavy traffic. "We blend old and new, East and West."

Lisa nodded. The longer she spent with Tuareg, the more the contrast in their own lives was apparent. He was used to cosmopolitan places like Soluddai. While she lived in a large city on America's west coast. She had a small, select group of friends. She had never been to London or Paris. Wasn't used to exotic sports cars. The gulf between them was never more pronounced.

For a moment she felt the gulf widen. It was impossible to stop, but she longed for some bridge that would enable the two of them to draw close. She knew he'd never forget his wife. She wouldn't fit in, she never had. But if they could only be friends—she'd be happy with that.

She could forget that the man she'd met in the desert

was Arabian royalty, used to servants and homes in three different countries. When it was the two of them, for short periods of time they could just be Tuareg and Lisa with no past or future.

"You've grown quiet," Tuareg said after a few moments.

"Thinking of how to outline the book," she lied. Suddenly the day didn't seem as bright as it had. Heartache lay around the corner. She wouldn't race to meet it, but it was inevitable. She'd fallen in love with a man so far out of her reach people would laugh if they learned the truth.

He turned into a large green park and stopped near the gates.

"Come, I'll show you one of the treasures of the park."

Walking along a path lined with shrubs and small flowering plants, Lisa saw puddles from the previous night's rain. The day was beautiful, not a cloud in the sky.

"Did you hear last night's storm?" she asked.

"Yes. Did it waken you?"

"It did. I was glad not to be out in it."

"Here." They came out of the shrubs into a wide grassy area. In the center was a statue twice as large as life.

It depicted a camel and a man in Arab dress both done in gleaming white marble.

"It's beautiful," she said, pausing to take it in. The man was looking toward the mountains. The camel was heavily laden with packs, stoically plodding at the man's shoulder.

"What's it about?" she asked, snapping pictures.

"He represents Mohammad bin Ker-Al. Two centuries ago a band of soldiers was fighting to the north. They were cut off from their supply lines and death was expected. They fought bravely. Then on the darkest night, Mohammad made his way through with a single camel loaded with critical supplies, enabling the soldiers to live another day. By that time, reinforcements reached the battleground and the tide of the war turned. Mohammad was from Soluddai. The city honors him."

She could almost imagine the scene. The professor should see this and hear the tale.

She circled the statue still a few dozen yards away. She needed that distance to capture the full scene in her lens.

"Who carved it?" she asked.

Tuareg gave her the name of the artist and a bit of his history. "He died young. This was his most impressive work," he finished.

"It is impressive. I think I could make this the cover photograph of my book."

Tuareg had always had a secret fascination with Mohammad bin Saladar, the artist. He had other work in museums and one in front of a school. To be able to carve such creations from a solid block of stone amazed him. He wondered if the artist felt an affinity for the hero, both sharing the same name.

Even though the man had died before he'd turned thirty, he'd left a legacy generations revered.

Tuareg wondered what lasting legacy he'd leave. The dam, for one. It would not be looked upon quite like this sculpture, but it would make a difference for future generations.

He would have liked to have children. Nura had not been ready. Each time he suggested it, she'd countered with how young they were and how much she wanted to do before they had children.

Now they never would.

He still stood near the path. Lisa had moved to take

pictures from different angles. Did she ever think to marry and have children? Or was she bitten by wanderlust and too busy capturing images on film to create a real life for herself? From her interaction with the children at the nomad settlement, he could tell she liked them. He suspected she would make a good mother. For the first time in three years, Tuareg wondered if he could hope for a different future.

CHAPTER NINE

WHEN THEY RETURNED to the car, he suggested lunch. "We can see more of the city later, if you wish," he said.

"Fine with me."

Heading for the villa, he glanced at Lisa from time to time. She was so very unlike Nura. She didn't demand attention. Didn't have to have constant activity to be content. The drive was completed in almost total silence, yet he didn't feel any awkwardness.

She was relaxing to be with, as well as intriguing. An interesting combination. Were other women as easy to spend time with?

He'd called ahead and when they arrived lunch was ready to be served on the patio. They sat where they had before, only there was no wheelchair this time.

"It's so beautiful," she said.

The salad was crisp and cool. The rolls crusty and hot.

"Do you regret we didn't prepare the meal?" he asked as she took her first bite.

She grinned at him and shook her head. "I couldn't compete with this. It's so good."

They talked desultorily through lunch. When finished, Lisa asked if she could tour the villa. And would he permit photographs of the garden?

Tuareg hesitated. He valued his privacy. But a few photographs of a generic garden couldn't hurt.

"Film them without the house as a background," he said.

"Deal."

"Come, I'll show you through the house," he said, rising.

Lisa slung her camera over her shoulder and followed Tuareg. They went to the grand foyer and stopped. The marble floor was cool, the wallpaper a pale champagne color. An expensive chandelier hung from the ceiling. The home looked like a model for a fancy magazine.

"The chandelier came from France," Tuareg said. He led the way into the salon. Lisa followed, stopping at the door. She'd glanced in at this room when she stayed here before. It was decorated entirely in shades of yellow. Light yellow, deep yellow, everything looked similar. The only other colors were the deep tones of the wood of some of the furniture.

She was at a loss to find complimentary words. She didn't like it at all. She much preferred a more colorful setting.

"A bit formal," Tuareg said, looking around as if seeing it for the first time. "I rarely use the room."

"If you don't use it, why not change it to be how you'd like?" Lisa asked.

For a moment the question startled him. "Nura decorated it."

"In fact, the entire villa seems too large for one man. If you truly don't expect to marry again, why not sell it to a family which would fill it up. Don't you think the house deserves children laughing in the hallway, sneaking into the kitchen at night to get a snack? Or running around the garden. Can't you picture it? With maybe a dog barking as he ran with them and a cat curled up in the windowsill?"

He frowned. "I don't picture the house that way. I do not wish to sell it. It reminds me of my wife. Why would I wish to cut that memory away?"

"You'll always remember her, Tuareg," Lisa said gently. "You don't need things for that. Did she never change anything?"

"She was always changing things. This is the third rendition of this room. Once it was all done in pale greens. She would live with each decor for a while, then start over again."

He remembered how excited she'd get when she'd find materials or accessories to redo one of the rooms. He'd joked with her more than once that it was a good thing they had such a large house, it gave her enough rooms to play with. The thought brought an ache. But not the sharp pain he was used to.

For a moment, he also remembered arguing with her about her redecorating because of boredom. They were never home long enough to get tired of the rooms before she changed them. Nura had argued back that when it was perfect, she'd know it and not need to redo it again. Perfection had constantly eluded her, however.

"I didn't mean to make you angry," Lisa said.

He crossed to the window. The garden was in full bloom, the blossoms drooping heavily on their stems.

"I'm not angry." He turned, leaning against the sill. "I am satisfied with my life the way it is. My wife is dead. She won't ever be with me again. I know that. I've made a new life. It is different than the old, but suits me as it is. I do not wish to change the house."

"I never meant you should, only if you wanted it a bit different. I'd like to see some more rooms if you'll still show me."

They visited each room on the first floor. The dining room was huge, with chairs enough for twenty. Lisa tried to envision a dinner party that large. She preferred smaller gatherings where she could converse with all her guests.

He hesitated at a door off the foyer, then opened it and stepped aside.

The small sitting room was a jewel—with bright colors of crimson and navy and white. The furniture looked as if it had been designed for comfort, not looks. She stepped inside. So the salon was for elegance. Was this a family sitting room? A place where they had been informal, a place to relax together when no guests were present?

"This is so darling," she said. She itched to take some pictures. It was elegant yet warm—almost a friendly room.

She looked at Tuareg. He stared at the sofa, then looked reluctantly around the room.

"She loved this room most of all," he said softly.

"I can see why. The wide windows allow all the beauty of the garden to come in," Lisa said. She sensed a strong emotion in him and moved to the windows to give him some privacy.

"He still loves you," she mentally said to a long-gone Nura.

If he hadn't gotten over his wife in three years, it was unlikely he would this summer. And in any case, he'd never fall for someone like her.

Lisa felt empty. She wanted to return to the dig and forget the feelings Tuareg caused. Try to forget secret dreams and wishes that they could find a common ground.

It was time to face reality and get back to her life. The fairy-tale existence of Arabia wasn't for a practical photographer from Seattle.

Lisa was back at the dig before lunch the next day. She had not seen Tuareg that morning. The museum had sent a Jeep to drive her back. She didn't know if he planned to visit the apartment before she left, but only Maliq was there to wish her well.

After briefing the professor, she went straight to work. Everyone was still excited about the recent discovery. More bones had been found, as well as some small decorative items that looked like some kind of jewelry. The piece that caught Lisa's fancy was a small leaf made of a delicate translucent green.

"Is that jade?" Lisa asked in astonishment when she first saw it.

"We think so," the professor said proudly. "It needs to be authenticated. If so, this proves a connection with the silk road. Not only a north and south route, but now a connection to the Orient. It was with one of the bodies we uncovered."

"Wow." Even Lisa knew what importance that could add to the excavation. Would this mean they'd get their deadline extended?

"Too early to make a definitive claim, but we are fairly certain," the professor said.

She took pictures from several angles. The pale color showed up well against the dark background she used.

The rest of the day passed like any other for Lisa. But the buzz of excitement couldn't be hidden among the archeologists.

By time dinner was served, Lisa felt more left out

than she usually did. She wasn't knowledgeable enough to discuss the implications of the recent find. She didn't have any close ties with members of the team. While they were all friendly enough, the new discovery was too exciting for them to indulge in idle chitchat. Sitting at one side of the group, she decided to take a walk after she finished eating.

She wandered to where the makeshift corral had been set up for Tuareg's horse. What fun it would be to mount up and ride beneath the growing moonlight. The landscape had a silvery aspect everywhere she looked—as if the world had changed to black and white. With the moon almost full, the stars weren't as bright, more like faint pinpricks of light on the black sky.

As far as she was concerned, this was the best time of day. The blazing heat had faded. The cool of dawn was hours away. She liked being outside at night.

Everywhere she looked reminded her of Tuareg. Was this how he felt at his home? Every sight a new reminder of his wife and what could never be? Most of Lisa's memories were her own, not shared with others. Sighing softly, she turned toward her tent. She'd bring her journal up to date and see about getting to bed early tonight.

She'd already developed the pictures she'd taken in Soluddai and gone through them several times, selecting the ones she wanted to include in her book. She loved the statue in the park the best.

And the one she'd caught of Tuareg as he leaned against his car waiting for her at one point during their day together.

The next morning Lisa was at the trench when one of the helpers ran over to her.

"There is a call for you in the main tent," he said breathlessly. "From Sheikh Tuareg al Shaldor."

Lisa almost ran to the tent, afraid he'd hang up if she didn't answer quickly.

"Hello?"

"Tuareg here. My uncle wishes to have a farewell dinner honoring the members of the excavation team the last Friday in August. Everything will be packed by then, correct?"

"I guess. I'd have to double-check a calendar." So much for the professor's hope that the deadline would be extended.

"Rooms will be obtained for everyone at the Luxor Hotel," he said.

Lisa knew it was the most expensive hotel in the capital city.

"How nice. Shouldn't you be talking to Professor Sanders about this?" she asked, puzzled by why Tuareg was calling her.

"Perhaps, but I wished to speak to you."

She sat on the stool nearby and smiled. "I'm glad to talk with you," she returned. Closing her eyes, she could picture him nearby.

"Have you been back to the desert?" she asked.

"I leave tomorrow for a few days. Ham will grow bored if not ridden occasionally. What have you been doing?"

"I developed all the photos I took in Soluddai. I'm uncertain now which ones to include for a book, however. I think I want something more. I love the picture of the statue. And some of the old architecture. For an American audience, I need more—something to capture the imagination."

"Such as?"

"I'm not sure. I hope I recognize it when I see it. We've had a most astonishing discovery here," she continued.

"Beyond the grave site?" he asked.

"They found a jade carving. To the professor it proves a connection with the silk road."

"Is he sure it is jade?"

"No, it needs to be authenticated. But like the porcelain statues, it lends strong credence to the possibility. It was discovered in the grave. Everyone here is quite excited."

"A find of major importance," Tuareg said thoughtfully.

"That's what they say. I've filmed it. It's quite delicate and lovely, very pale green with a translucence that looked ethereal."

"Are you equally thrilled?"

She laughed softly. "I'm not fully aware of all the ramifications. And finding such a treasure doesn't offer me the opportunity for increased fame as it does the professor. According to some of the students here, once it becomes known he's made such a major find, he'll be sought after for other digs. And it means more prestige at the university for him."

"But not for you?"

"I'm just the photographer. Thank you again for taking me to your villa the other day. I also have some terrific shots of the gardens. Maybe I'll do a book on gardens near and far one day. I could get in photos for Butchart Gardens in Vancouver, Kew Gardens in London and the Tuileries in France to add to the one with the statue of your hero."

"Ambitious indeed. When will you return to Soluddai?"

"Probably not until after we pack up for home," she said. For a moment she hoped he'd invite her to visit again.

"Will you be at the party your uncle is having?"

"Of course. We can also celebrate the resumption of work on the dam."

She sighed. He put such importance on the new construction—while her focus was on the past. "Then I'll hope to see you there."

"Lisa—"

"Yes?"

There was a pause, then Tuareg merely said, "Take care of yourself. I'll see you before you return to America."

Hanging up the phone she wished she could have found something scintillating to hold his interest. No matter how often she told herself there could be nothing between them, there was a small bud of hope deep within her that cried out for Tuareg.

Two days later three Jeeps arrived at the camp carrying men from the National Museum. Lisa heard them and went out of the tent to see who was visiting. In the lead Jeep was the minister of antiquities. Surprised to see more than a dozen men arrive unannounced, she went to greet the minister. At least she recognized him.

"Professor Sanders is here?" he asked when he'd acknowledged her greeting.

"At the trench. I can show you the way."

He barked out some instructions to the others. Two men went into the work tent, two came to walk with him, the others began unloading items from the vehicles.

Lisa glanced at them warily as they walked to the hole in the ground. "Is something wrong?" she asked.

"Nothing that concerns you," he snapped. In only moments they reached the steps that led to the lower level where the current excavation was taking place.

With the latest discovery spurring them on, the archeologists had renewed enthusiasm and embraced the longer days the professor had decreed. They were up and at the site by the time Lisa arose each morning.

Lunch breaks were staggered and dinner was late each night as they used as much daylight as possible.

"Professor Sanders?" she called.

He came around one of the corners. "Yes?" He didn't know the minister so Lisa made the introductions.

"I'm delighted you came to see the site," the professor said.

"We have come to do more than see it. As of today I am officially taking charge of the excavation. You and your team will pack your things and leave. We expect the site to be vacated by tomorrow afternoon," the minister said.

"What?" The professor was astonished. Work stopped as everyone turned to look at the tableau unfolding.

"We have until the end of the summer," Professor Sanders said.

"That has changed. I need you to show me what you've found since the shipment to the museum and then begin packing. My men will take over. The importance of the site has increased and we wish to be in charge."

"What happened to change things?" the professor asked.

"I believe a discovery of some importance has recently been made. A jade piece."

"We suspect it is jade. It needs to be authenticated."

"Which will change the entire history of the area. It is too important to leave to others. Our own historians will continue."

"But—"

"No more. Please, ask the members of your group to leave the site. We prefer you not mention any discoveries of this summer to anyone. We will release information to the world at the appropriate time."

Lisa watched, stunned. How had the minister heard about the jade?

Suddenly she felt sick. Had her sharing the discovery with Tuareg led to this? The look on the professor's face would stay with her a long time. He'd poured his heart and soul into this dig. They couldn't just snatch it away from him without any warning. Or take away his part in all the work this summer.

Turning, she hurried back to the work tent. She ignored the men now putting all the artifacts into cartons and went straight to the phone. She picked it up, then hesitated. She hadn't a clue how to contact Tuareg. But if anyone could stop the steamroller techniques of the minister, it would be him.

"Excuse me," she said, turning to the strangers. "Does anyone speak English?"

"I do," the younger man said.

"Could you please help me call someone?"

"Yes." He walked over. "Who do you wish to call?"

"Sheikh Tuareg al Shaldor."

The man blinked, then gingerly took the phone. He quickly connected with an operator and spoke rapidly. A few moments later he bowed slightly and handed Lisa the phone.

"Tuareg?" she said.

"I'm sorry, ma'am," a feminine voice answered. "His Excellency is not in the city at this time. Can someone else be of assistance?"

"Has he gone to the desert?"

"Who is this?"

"Lisa Sullinger. Is he in the desert?"

"I'm afraid the whereabouts of His Excellency are not for public knowledge. If I could take a message, I'll see he gets it when he returns."

"That'll be too late." Lisa hung up.

Dammit, there had to be some way to reach Tuareg. He would help, she knew it.

Could she find Tuareg's camp?

She had enlisted the professor's help one evening in reviewing local maps and deciding where other ruins might be located. She'd wanted to take more photographs—the last days of the Moquansaid plains—highlighting abandoned homes wherever she found them; picturing the oasis that would be underwater by this time next year.

She knew the location of the house where she'd fallen. Could she find Tuareg's camp from there? She had a vague memory of the way. Would it be enough?

She went to the large table holding maps and glanced through them until she found one that showed the old house. Studying it, she didn't see any other markings indicating a camp or settlement. But wouldn't he have set up the tent where there was nothing else? He wanted to be alone, not where others might stumble across the tent.

The professor entered the tent, glancing at the men working and then looked at Lisa.

"I'm afraid our expedition is over. I've asked for three days to pack up and arrange transportation. Not much time, but more than tomorrow's deadline."

"I tried to reach Tuareg, but he's not there. I think he's at his tent. If you'd let me borrow one of the Jeeps, I believe I can find him. He'd be able to stop this." She hated to admit her possible part in the Ministry of Antiquities learning about the jade. If she'd caused this situation, she better do all she could to get them out of it.

"Where is the tent located?"

"West of the old ruins where I fell. I can get there easily enough and then head west. I think I'll remember landmarks to help me," she said.

"You could get lost out there. It's too dangerous. We'll put in a call to His Excellency and see if we can come to some agreement."

Lisa watched as the professor went to place a call. Tapping her fingers on the table, she knew the moment his request had been denied by his expression.

Turning, she took the keys from the rack where they normally were kept and, stopping only long enough to get some bottles of water and some snack food, she climbed in the first Jeep and headed out.

This vehicle had GPS positioning and she hoped it would be enough to get her back if she couldn't find Tuareg.

She treated the desert with more respect after the sandstorm. But this was too important to delay.

By late morning she could make out the outline of several buildings and tall palms silhouetted against a clear blue sky. She'd found the old dwelling. She stopped briefly and got out to see if she could find tracks from Ham. But if they were there, they were covered over. The wind might not have been as strong as during the sandstorm, but it was consistent and would have easily erased all traces of the horse's passing.

She'd have to rely on her memory of that ride.

Having jotted the coordinates, she turned and began driving west.

By mid afternoon, Lisa was almost ready to return to camp. She was lost. The Jeep could easily cover twice the ground a horse would travel at a walk in the hours she'd been driving. She stopped the vehicle and, standing on the seat, she searched in a complete circle. Nothing.

Of course, she could be near the tent and have a hard time seeing it, it blended with the land. But she'd surely see trees denoting an oasis. There were none to be seen.

It was almost too hot to think.

It had been more than a week since Lisa had last seen Tuareg, but only a couple of days since they talked. Had he caused their expulsion?

Lisa was tired. She wished she could find some shade and lie down and take a nap. But she sat back in the driver's seat and started the Jeep again. Checking the gas gauge, she still had more than half a tank. Once she reached the halfway point, she'd have to return to camp.

Lisa turned north and drove for a half hour. Checking again, she saw nothing that looked familiar. Time was running out. If she didn't find Tuareg, they had three days to pack up and leave. She knew she couldn't cover the entire area. The distances were too great. But if she didn't find him today, she'd go out again tomorrow and the next day and search as far each day as she could.

Lisa stopped once more. The gas gauge registered half. She would drive back in a straighter line using the GPS device than she'd taken coming this far, but didn't want to risk being stuck in the desert.

Once more she scanned the horizon. Wait—there, to the north, those were palm trees. Was that where Tuareg camped?

She drove as fast as the Jeep would go over the rough

terrain. Almost bouncing out of the Jeep at one point, she slowed. Now that she thought she was almost there, she could hardly wait.

Soon she saw the trees, then the tent's roof. As soon as she reached the tent, she stopped the engine and jumped out.

"Tuareg?" she called. She raced to the opening, stepping inside. It was Tuareg's tent, she recognized every fantastic piece inside. But it was empty.

Was he riding Ham?

She could scarcely breathe. Was he coming back? Or had he left to return to the city? She ran outside and around to the corral where the horse stayed. There was fresh water and hay stacked outside the rails. He was coming back, she thought. She hoped.

Walking slowly back to the Jeep, she climbed in and reached for a bottle of water. It was tepid, but wet. Sipping, she kept watch. He had to be returning.

CHAPTER TEN

TUAREG RETURNED TO his tent near dusk. He and Ham had ridden a long distance, but the horse was still full of energy. It was Tuareg who was tired.

As he crested a knoll, he saw a Jeep at the tent. Too far away to see who was sitting in it, he became wary. Few people knew where he erected the tent. Was there an emergency?

"Tuareg!" Lisa called when he was still some distance away. She climbed out of the Jeep and started running toward him.

He urged Ham to a faster gait and in only a short time pulled in beside her, dismounting.

"What are you doing here?" he asked, surprised to see her. Surprised at the feelings seeing her brought. He wanted to pull her into his arms and make sure she was safe. Her face was red with sunburn. Glancing beyond her, he saw the Jeep. Had she come all this way alone? It was dangerous in the desert for someone who didn't know it well.

"Tuareg, something terrible has happened and I need you to make it right," she said, clinging to his arm. "Please."

"What's wrong?"

"Your minister of antiquities arrived at camp this morning and ordered us to leave."

He began walking toward the tent, holding the reins, Ham following.

"I know," he said.

"You know?" She stopped and stared at him. "Did you send him?"

"No, my uncle sent him. But I told him about the jade discovery. The porcelain figurines caused a lot of interest when they were unpacked. With the latest find, the site takes on new meaning."

"Professor Sanders was heartbroken when ordered to leave. He's put a lot into this excavation. He can't just be sent away. He deserved credit for the discoveries."

Tuareg kept silent. The ins and outs of the situation didn't greatly concern him. His uncle had made the order.

"Tuareg, please help us."

"It's not my responsibility to change my uncle's orders," he said. They reached the rails where he kept Ham. He unsaddled the horse and turned him loose in the enclosure. There was plenty of water. Tuareg forked some hay in and turned.

He almost bumped into Lisa. He drew a deep breath. He hadn't wanted to see her again. He didn't like the feelings that were building whenever she was around.

He'd never thought to get involved with another woman. He didn't want to be. There was too much risk of another death. Another crushing heartbreak that would alter life forever.

He knew it was cowardice, but he couldn't bring himself to open up to the desolation such a loss brought.

No one understood. His mother urged him to get

out and meet other women. As if Nura had been one of several and all he had to do was go pick a new model.

Lisa put her hand on her arm, looking up at him. "I'm asking you to help us. Help Professor Sanders. I need you to make it come right. I'm the one who told you about the jade. That's what it's all about, isn't it? If I'd kept quiet, none of this would have happened."

"The porcelain pieces sparked their interest. Those set the thing in motion. Discovery of jade only hastened the end."

"So you won't help me?"

He started to say no, then reconsidered.

"I'll make no promises, but I'll contact my uncle."

"Oh, thank you, Tuareg," Lisa said, throwing her arms around his neck and pulling his face down for a kiss.

He responded with alacrity, gathering her in his arms and turning the thank you peck into a full-blown kiss. The heat of the sun could not rival the heat that exploded within the embrace. She clung and he drew her closer, wishing never to let go. If he let himself think of the danger she'd faced, alone in the desert, it would chill his blood. He wanted her always laughing with eyes sparkling.

Slowly, they pulled apart. She was breathing hard. He was, too. She looked so full of hope his heart twisted. For one blinding moment, he wished she'd want him with the same passion she displayed for saving Professor Sanders's position.

"I told you no guarantees," he said, before she came to expect the impossible.

"I know. But at least you'll try. Thank you."

He strode into the tent and went to the radio. Lisa followed and sat on the divan, watching as if he could do no wrong. He'd been the one to tell his uncle about the jade and the hypothesis of the connection to the silk road. His uncle had immediately set in motion the rescinding of the permit for the archeologists.

Tuareg could feel the suppressed expectation shimmering from her as she steadily watched him. The result of his conversation with his uncle was not going to be the one she hoped for.

"I understand," he told the older man. The events set in motion would not be halted. The archeological team would have to leave.

He turned away, not wanting to see the disappointment on her face. Soon enough he'd have to confront that.

"I will personally go to the camp and make sure things go as you wish," he told his uncle.

He hung up.

"Well?" she asked.

Slowly he turned. He shrugged out of his robes and went to the cooler to get a cold drink. "Do you want something to drink?" he asked.

"He said no, didn't he," she said, drooping with disappointment.

"He said no," Tuareg confirmed. He hated to see her so unhappy. She looked so defeated sitting there.

"You have the pictures you took. The notebooks," he said.

She shook her head. "They took all my pictures as well. I hope to get the ones back that aren't of the site, but even that's not certain." She went outside. He heard her cross the ground and then the sound of the Jeep.

Was she leaving? Quickly he followed, reaching the flap as the engine started.

"It'll be dark soon," he said, hurrying toward the Jeep.

"I have headlights," she said, backing around.

"Wait and I'll go with you."

"What for?" she said. "We'll pack and be gone in three days. We don't need you there."

"You came to me for help."

"Which you didn't deliver."

"Lisa, it's not my decision."

"Maybe not, but it's my fault you learned about the jade. What an idiot I've been. The professor will probably hate me for telling you." She glared at him. "And you for telling others."

He reached the Jeep and held on to the edge. "Let me go with you. I can try to get your photographs back."

She didn't respond immediately.

"I need to take care of a few things. I can be ready to leave in ten minutes."

Before she could reply, he reached across and turned off the engine, pulling out the key.

She glared at him. "Looks like I have no choice."

"Ten minutes."

Tuareg went to the tent and gathered what he'd need to stay a few days at the camp. He contacted one of his employees to instruct him to come care for Ham. He was ready in less than the ten minutes promised. He couldn't change his uncle's decree, but he could mitigate the situation. And make sure Lisa got her pictures back—all of them.

When he reached the Jeep, Lisa hadn't moved.

"I'll drive," he said.

She shrugged and slid over to the passenger side.

Tuareg glanced at the GPS indicator. "Is that set for the camp?"

She nodded.

"Lisa," he said in exasperation, "not talking to me won't change a thing."

"Yes, it is set to the camp."

"I'm surprised you found me," Tuareg said, starting the engine.

"It wasn't easy. You'll see we're right at halfway on gas. If I hadn't seen the palm trees on my last survey of the horizon, I would have headed back and tried again tomorrow."

Tuareg glanced at her as the Jeep bounced over the uneven ground. "If something had gone wrong, you could have been in serious trouble going off like that. What if you had not found me and gotten a flat tire or something?"

"I didn't," she said.

"I know. But the desert is a dangerous place."

She sighed softly and looked around her. "Maybe, but I think it is also a place of beauty. Being here has shown me a whole different way of life. I may consider moving from Seattle when I return home."

"To?"

"Arizona, New Mexico—one of the desert states." She'd toyed with the idea for a while now. She loved the clear sunshine, the way rocks and land changed color with the sun's travels. She'd miss Bailey and Sara and her other friends if she moved, but she would always have their friendship and she'd make more friends wherever she settled.

The thought of a flat-roofed home with terra-cotta walls blending with the landscape held great appeal. She'd love to see the shimmering colors of the desert come alive each day.

"Not everyone likes the desert. Or they grow tired of it after a time," Tuareg said.

"Hmm," she said, drinking from one of the bottles of water she'd brought along. "Do you?"

He shook his head. "I was born here, of a line of people who have lived in Moquansaid forever. It's a part of me."

"Yet your villa is lush with vegetation, flowers and flowing water."

"I like an occasional oasis in the desert, don't you?"

She nodded. "That's part of the unexpected appeal of the place, the contrasts. I think I could have lived in Wadi Hirum. Only I would have built my house closer to the river."

"Maybe the river flowed closer to the settlement five hundred years ago," he said.

"There's a thought," she said.

As they bounced along, Lisa wished she didn't feel like a traitor to the professor. Once or twice the Jeep swerved around a clump of grass, feeling as if it might continue in a rollover. She gasped and clutched the edge of the Jeep.

"I won't wreck the car," Tuareg said.

"My mother didn't think she'd wreck the car, but accidents happen," Lisa said, feeling her heart pounding. She liked dry, straight roads.

"Is that how she died, in a car crash?"

"Yes."

He glanced at her. "How old were you?"

"Six. I was with her."

He looked startled at that. Lisa wondered why she'd told him. She hadn't spoken of that night in a long time.

"Were you hurt?"

"No, but I was pinned in the car, my foot was caught.

It was pouring rain. Cold. Dark. I kept calling for my mother, but she never answered." Lisa couldn't help shivering in memory. That horror would never completely fade.

"What happened?"

His calm tone helped her get past the emotional flashback and respond in an equally calm tone.

"After what seemed like forever, another car came along and stopped. Then it was a trip to the hospital for me and my father came for me. A couple of bones in my foot were broken. The same foot injured during the sandstorm."

"You never get over something like that."

"No." They drove in silence for a while.

"Were you with your wife when she died?" she asked. His mother had said she'd had an aneurysm.

"It was a family gathering. We were at the table eating when she screamed in pain. Everyone looked instantly, but before I could react, she fell back, slid off her chair to the floor. By the time I got to her, she was dead."

"I'm sorry for your loss."

"And for yours."

Lisa would have thought the common loss of loved ones might bring them closer together, but Tuareg seemed to withdraw within himself after telling her about his wife's death.

It was late by the time the lights from camp were seen. When they arrived, Professor Sanders came out of the work tent.

"We were growing worried about you, Lisa. Your Excellency, is there anything you can do for us?" he asked Tuareg.

"I cannot change the ministry being in charge now. But Lisa told me about the order to keep the discoveries quiet. You pushed for the excavation, you have found the items of major interest. You will get credit for that. And I need to talk to the man. He has no rights to Lisa's photographs."

"I'm not so interested in credit as in what else might be discovered. These artifacts will alter the way we view history in this part of the world," Professor Sanders said.

Tuareg climbed out of the Jeep and went to the work tent. Lisa watched him disappear inside then looked at the professor. "I'm sorry, I really thought he could make it right."

"There are lots of disappointments in life. But we all move on. I'm glad you got back safely." He turned and walked slowly toward his private tent.

Lisa went to the mess tent to get something to eat. Checking the shower schedule, she saw it was free and quickly signed her name to the board. Everyone else was talking in small groups and generally complaining about things. She'd never have a better time for a quick wash.

The shower was nothing like a real one. The water was gathered in large tanks suspended from a high platform. During the day the sun heated it. By early evening it was warm enough to enjoy.

She gathered her towel and some clean shorts and a shirt and headed for the shower stall some distance away from the camp. The wooden platform where bathers stood had wide slats which allowed the water to drain away in the desert. Several plants had blossomed with the unexpected treat of water over the last few weeks.

The shower was enclosed on all sides by canvas panels. Lisa sometimes wished they'd have one facing away from camp be clear plastic so she'd have a view while she bathed.

As she crossed the compound, Tuareg joined her.

"Your pictures are being segregated and will be returned to you in the morning. I also insisted on the negatives. You are allowed to take one copy of each of the notebooks. If you choose to give them to the professor, that's your privilege."

"Oh, Tuareg, thank you. So he will have a complete set of all that was discovered here this summer?"

He nodded. "Were you going for a walk?" he asked.

"I'm headed to take a shower."

"And it's that way?"

"It's not plumbed, just gravity fed. And a bit away to assure privacy."

"Then I'll walk with you."

When the canvas structure came into view, Lisa wondered if he planned to wait while she showered.

She glanced at Tuareg. As ever, he was watching her. The light was fading, but she thought she saw a glimmer of amusement.

When they reached the shower, he studied it for a moment, then glanced around. "No bench?"

"What for?"

"For people to wait."

"We sign up for times, no waiting."

"I'll wait for you."

The thought of disrobing and showering with only a piece of canvas between them had Lisa growing warm all over. It seemed very intimate.

She walked to the opening. There were hooks on the

wooden frame for clothing and towels. She hung her clean clothes and the towel. Taking her soap and shampoo from her small bag, she placed them where she could reach them. She peered around. There was no one in sight. Still she hesitated to disrobe. But the minutes were ticking by and her time slot could be shortened if someone else came.

Before she could change her mind, she swiftly took off her clothes and stepped beneath the high shower head. Pulling the cord, she tied it in place as the warm water caressed her skin. She turned it off to lather her hair.

"Finished already?" His voice came from just on the other side of the canvas. Lisa jumped.

"No, we don't waste water. I'm soaping up."

"Ahh."

She shivered. "You're making me nervous," she exclaimed.

"Why is that?"

She bit her lip, pulling the cord and letting the water wash over her. "I'm not used to…to company while I bathe."

She heard him laugh softly. Her lips turned up involuntarily.

"An interesting tidbit to file away," he said.

"Go take a walk," she said.

"I won't go far," he replied.

She strained to hear, but couldn't tell if he walked away or not.

Speeding through her wash, she soon wrapped her towel around her and dried off. The clean clothes felt wonderful. She combed through her hair, but left it to dry in the arid air. It would be by the time she reached her tent.

Gathering her things, she stepped around the enclosure. There was no one nearby, so he had walked away.

She headed for the compound. When she drew close to her tent, she looked for Tuareg. There was no sign of him.

Tuareg stayed in the shadows watching to make sure Lisa returned safely to her tent. What was he going to do about Lisa? Instead of another month before she would leave, his uncle had moved up their timetable. She could be gone as early as the day after tomorrow.

He knew that each night as he tried to sleep, the thought of Lisa would surface. He could picture her joy in taking pictures. Her enthusiasm in preserving for the present places of the past. He could imagine her carefully framing each picture to give it the best showing, the care she'd take on her book.

It was like her to think of making a book of the plain as it was today and would never again be. He'd be interested in seeing such a book.

He wrestled with the longing to go to her, hear her laughter, be enchanted by her grin.

But could he let Nura go and fall in love with someone else? It always came back to that.

He'd been afraid today when he thought of Lisa going off on her own and traveling where there was no help to be found. If she'd had a flat tire or blown an engine part, she could have been totally stranded. How long would a search team have taken to find her?

Would he ever have learned of her death? The thought appalled him. Was it already too late to turn away?

CHAPTER ELEVEN

TIME DID NOT STAND STILL. Two days remained before Lisa had to leave. Then Tuareg would say goodbye to Lisa Sullinger. She'd return to Seattle, he'd return to his empty villa.

"When is the best time to visit Seattle?" he asked.

"What?" she said. She was sitting on her cot looking at the photographs, trying to ascertain if the minister had returned all she'd taken. Tuareg sat near the table watching her.

"What season is your best in Seattle?" he repeated.

"Summer, I guess. Though it rains a lot. Still, it's gorgeous when it's dry. You planning to visit?"

"Maybe."

"I have to tell you if you wait until next summer, I may be gone."

That startled him. "Gone where?"

"I don't know, but I've really enjoyed my summer here and thought I'd apply again for one of the expeditions. Jamie said they might be able to get one going near Damascus. Or maybe I'll sign on for one in Mexico. Imagine, hot and humid. I'd probably hate the weather but be as fascinated by the discoveries as I was here."

She had another life. One that didn't include him. She wouldn't be sitting in her apartment awaiting his visit. Tuareg rose and paced the small interior.

"What are you doing?" she said looking up at him.

"Nothing." He stopped.

"I'm almost done."

What would things be like when she was gone?

He wasn't sure he wanted to even speculate. Maybe he should seriously consider visiting Seattle before next summer.

"What do you think?" she asked, holding up a picture of the statue in the park.

He forced himself to study the photographs when everything inside him suddenly wanted to ask her to stay.

Lisa sat on a box and watched as the tents were struck. Her personal items had been boxed up yesterday. She'd packaged most of her pictures to be shipped home from Soluddai, but was carrying all the negatives. One or the other was bound to reach Seattle.

Jaime and Paul had left with half the crew to facilitate the loading of the equipment at the shipping terminal in Soluddai. Professor Sanders and the rest were scampering around, making sure everything was taken care of. Her work was finished. She'd shot a couple of last-minute pictures for the memory books, double-checked on everyone's address and now had nothing to do but sit and watch.

Tuareg had left with the truck carrying their equipment. He'd offered to return to fly her to Soluddai, but she'd declined. She wanted this time with her summer companions. After the flight in two days, she wouldn't see most of them again. The professor, maybe. She'd already spoken to him about another expedition.

She watched, trying to keep her mind a blank. She was staying at Yasmin's apartment tomorrow night after the reception. Then early the next morning they'd all board a plane, head for Rome and then home. She would not think about it. She'd take each moment as it came and not dwell on the goodbyes that were inevitable.

Lisa was used to goodbyes, but she never liked them. Yet she knew better than most that relationships were fleeting.

The sun was hot. She blinked back tears. This time next year, water would cover the earth where she sat. The trees that had given them shade would be rotting. The traces of the people who had one time lived here would be gone forever. And the man she'd fallen in love with would ride his horse on the desert—alone. It was all sad.

But nothing was as sad as leaving Tuareg behind. She wished she were brave enough to tell him how she felt. Would knowing someone else loved him have him change his mind about taking a chance? She didn't think so. If she did, she'd risk it.

The reception was lavish. The grand hall of the museum had been thrown open to patrons of the museum, special guests and the members of Professor Sanders's archeological expedition. Lisa wore the same dress she'd bought for Jeppa's party. She saw the young woman shortly after arriving. Jeppa had greeted her with a friendly wave and later came to speak with her.

Yasmin had picked Lisa up at the hotel that morning and they'd spent the day in her flat. Lisa had met Tuareg's father and been charmed by him. She could see a lot of him in his son. Yasmin had not said if Tuareg still planned to attend the festivities or not.

Lisa glanced around the crowded room. There were several tall men with dark hair, but none were Tuareg. Each time she saw one, her heart skipped a beat. Disappointment followed when she didn't recognize the man.

Despite essentially being booted out of the country, Professor Sanders was the man of the hour. Even the minister was smiling. Lisa raised her camera to capture the moment. The final set of photos for the memory books, unless she took one tomorrow as they boarded the plane.

"And who takes your pictures for the memory book?" a dear familiar voice asked.

She turned, her heart leaping in gladness. "You do," she replied, handing him her camera.

Tuareg took several shots, one with her and the minister, who once again beamed his pleasure at the results of the excavation so far.

Lisa made a wry face when they moved away. "What a change from my bringing the first set of boxes," she murmured as Tuareg walked with her. She wished they could escape to quieter locations in the museum, spend these last hours together, just the two of them, instead of being with a group of two hundred.

"He is in very good favor with my uncle and it shows. Do you wish something to drink?"

"Yes, please." She should be angry at Tuareg for hastening their departure. For not finding in her what she found in him. But the fleeting moments were too precious. She'd hold on and let anger build tomorrow.

He summoned a circulating waiter and they both took glasses.

"To a bright future, Lisa Sullinger. May your book

bring you fame and fortune." He touched the rim of his glass to hers.

"Thank you," she said, looking away lest he see the gathering tears.

She wasn't sure she could do this—pretend she was having a good time when her heart was breaking. How much longer until the event ended? Could she pretend her ankle hurt and she needed to leave early?

"There you are, Lisa. Come with me. I have a friend I want you to meet," Jeppa said a moment later. "He's going to graduate school at Berkeley, but that's not that far from Seattle, is it? He could fly to visit you. He's a lot of fun." She linked arms with Lisa and escorted her away from Tuareg.

Lisa glanced over her shoulder and shrugged. Maybe it was best to stay busy. Keep the sad thoughts at bay.

"Lisa, this is Hamid. Hamid, Lisa is a famous photographer, I have one of her books." Jeppa made the introductions and encouraged them to exchange contact information.

Lisa smiled politely. Hamid looked to be about her age and was going for a specialty in medicine. He asked for Lisa's address and told her that once he was settled, he'd call her. When he saw another friend, she was left alone. Searching for Tuareg, Lisa couldn't see him. Had he left already? How much longer would the reception last?

The next morning, leaving her room was difficult because of the tears that ran down her face. She would mop her eyes, begin to leave, think of the final departure and the reality of saying goodbye would strike and she'd start crying again.

"For heaven's sake, get a grip," she admonished

herself, trying to stem the flow of tears. She could write to Yasmin. Learn about Tuareg from her letters.

It was infatuation. She'd get over him as soon as she became involved in other activities at home.

She had Hamid's visit to look forward to.

Tears started again. She bit her lip, took a breath and went to the bathroom to splash cold water on her face.

"Do not start again," she told her reflection.

It was not only Tuareg, though he was the one she'd miss the most. The thought of bidding everyone good-bye tore at her heart. She hated farewells. She'd spent her entire life leaving or being left. When did she get to stay? When did she get to be part of a family that would never go away or send her away?

"Maybe never. Suck it up and get this show on the road," she said. Taking another deep breath, she went back to the bedroom, gathered her camera and carry-on bag and left the suitcase for the maid to take to the car.

She thanked her hostess without more tears, though they were perilously close.

The drive to the airport was in the luxury of a limo. She watched the buildings of the city speed by. She had not spent her last days taking photos as she had originally planned. Maybe some day she'd come back and take more in the city then. If she ever came back to see the reservoir.

Once at the airport, she quickly found her friends. They checked bags, went through security and waited at the gate. The large jet would board soon.

Everyone was somber, sulky almost. No one talked. The flight was called and they queued up to board.

Lisa looked around one last time. She had hoped—her heart stopped, began to pound.

Tuareg was striding toward her. He'd come after all

to bid her goodbye. Last night he'd disappeared before she'd had a chance to tell him goodbye. She was so thankful he'd come today.

She darted out of line.

"Lisa?" Professor Sanders called in bewilderment.

"I'll be right there," she called back, heading for Tuareg.

"You came," she said when they met.

"I couldn't let you leave without saying goodbye."

"Thanks for everything." She couldn't say anything more. Her throat was closing. To her horror, her eyes filled with tears. They spilled down her cheek. She wanted to invite him to Seattle, to ask him to proof her book before the final submission, to tell him she loved him. Only the tears spilled faster than she could think. She caught back a sob.

"Ah, Lisa, don't cry. You break my heart."

She shook her head. His heart had broken when Nura died. And she guessed it would never heal again.

He pulled her gently into his embrace, holding her while the tears flowed. She felt safe. As she had when her father had held her so long ago. As she had during the sandstorm in a stranger's embrace. She would always feel safe in Tuareg's arms.

"Don't go," he said softly.

"What?" she asked, resting her forehead against his shoulder, breathing in the scent she remembered from that first day at the ruin when he had sheltered her from the storm's fury.

"Stay. With me. Don't go."

She hadn't heard him right. She had always had an abundant imagination. Now she was imagining what she wanted most to hear.

Slowly she pulled back until she could see his eyes,

dark and sad, they tugged at her heart. Passengers passed, one bumped her slightly, but she didn't notice. Another boarding call was made in three languages. Her time was limited. But she couldn't move an inch.

"Marry me, Lisa. Stay here in Moquansaid. Publish your book, find new subjects, only don't leave. I'll get you on a dig with local scholars. You can photograph the inside of every building anyone in my family owns. Take photos of every structure in the city."

She put her fingertips over his mouth. "Tuareg, are you crazy?"

"Only if I let you go. I realized that last night. When Jeppa introduced you to Hamid, I was struck by the thought of you with someone else. I couldn't bear that. I loved Nura. You know that. But I love you—differently, passionately, forever. You said once I could find another love. Not someone to replace her, but to succeed her. You are that someone. I fought against it. My mother and Jeppa suspected my feelings long before I did. I felt I was disloyal to Nura if I found another woman. But Nura was a generous woman. She loved me and wanted my happiness no matter what. She would be upset if she'd known how I cut myself off from new experiences for mourning her."

"I'm nothing like her," Lisa said.

"I don't want you to be. Your eyes change color. Now they are silvery and sad. Sometimes they are smoky blue. Other times gray. I'm always trying to figure out what makes them change. I could spend a lifetime figuring that out."

"Really?" She began to smile.

"They are growing blue," he said. "And your grin is infectious. I could watch your delight in things all day long. When you greeted me a few weeks ago at the camp, I knew I wanted you to show that same happiness when I returned home each day. To see you each morning, love you all night long, learn to cook together. Lisa, you have already enriched my life, I cannot imagine living the rest of it without you. Say you'll marry me. If you don't like Moquansaid, we can find a place we both like."

"I do like Moquansaid. I love the desert. And I'd love to marry you! Would we live in your tent?"

He laughed, picked her up and spun her around. Passengers stopped and stared. The man at the ticket counter called out something.

Tuareg replied in Arabic.

"What?" Lisa asked, looking over her shoulder. They were closing the door to the ramp leading to her plane. "My plane, I'm going to miss the plane."

"So? You've said you'll marry me. We'll fly to Seattle in a few days, pack up your things and ship them back here. Let that plane go. There are others."

She looked at him. "Are you sure?"

"That I love you? Yes. That you mean as much to me as Nura, that and more. She and I were children together. We knew each other so well. I loved her, but it was a love that had grown complaisant. With you everything is new and different. You fascinate me. You delight me. You make me so crazy with desire I'm a saint to resist sweeping you away and making love to you for a week. Say we can marry soon."

Lisa laughed. Tears dried on her cheeks. Her heart swelled with enchantment. "I have no family, only a few friends who could probably fly out here with a few days' notice, so there's no reason to wait—and every reason to hurry."

"Oh, and why is that?" he asked.

"I want our honeymoon at the tent—and we have to get there before the water rises. Oh, Tuareg, I love you so much!"

He pulled her tightly into his arms and kissed her.

EPILOGUE

LISA STOOD ON THE SHORE and gazed over the wide expanse of water. The sun was shining, as it usually did. There was a light breeze, enough to ruffle the surface of the reservoir. She couldn't see the other side. Despite her reservations, her thoughts of the ruins now flooded, the setting was beautiful.

She raised her camera and took a picture. Soon new plants and trees would grow, watered by the reservoir. She turned and spoke haltingly to the woman she'd come to visit. One of the nomads from her visit last summer. Her Arabic was still imperfect, but she practiced daily, speaking with all her new family, enduring their laughter and gentle smiles when she got something wrong.

She didn't care. She relished them all and they seemed to love her. She'd found her place in the world and loved every aspect of it.

"How do you like all the water?" she asked.

The woman looked at the neat rows that had been planted, green shoots already showing. "It is different. But it will be good. The men have the hardest time. They like to roam. Now we are staying."

Lisa took a picture of the neat parallel row of homes. The terra-cotta color as appealing to her today as when she first arrived. She lowered her camera and reached into her tote, pulling out a photograph of the woman and her children she'd taken on that first visit. She'd had it framed. She handed it to the woman, smiling at the expression of wonder on her face.

"It will be in a book that will be published next year," Lisa said. She was delighted with the way the book had come together. She and Tuareg had worked side by side in selecting the photographs. He'd put her in touch with a professor at the university in Soluddai who had added facts for each caption. The publisher of her previous books had been thrilled with the new work, claiming it would sell not only to the general population, but to universities as a study of what could be done before change took place. Lisa was delighted and already had an idea for another project.

"Thank you." The woman bowed, then smiled. "I wish you happiness," she said, gesturing to Lisa's stomach.

She was a month away from giving birth to their first baby. She grinned. "I have happiness, but thank you. It will only grow with this baby."

"What will grow?" Tuareg asked, coming to stand near her, surveying the rows of crops. She still thrilled every time she saw him. It was hard to believe they'd been married almost a year.

"Happiness," she said simply, knowing they would have an abundance of it for all their lives.

HARLEQUIN® *Romance*®

MEDITERRANEAN DADS

In the first of this emotional Mediterranean Dads duet, nanny Julie is whisked away to a palatial Italian villa, but she feels completely out of place in Massimo's glamorous world. Her biggest challenge, though, is ignoring her attraction to the brooding tycoon.

Look for

The Italian Tycoon and the Nanny

by **Rebecca Winters**

in March wherever you buy books.

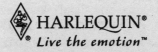

HARLEQUIN®
Live the emotion™

HARLEQUIN®

Mediterranean
NIGHTS™

*Things are heating up
aboard Alexandra's Dream....*

Coming in March 2008

ISLAND HEAT

by

Sarah Mayberry

It's been eight years since Tory Sanderson found
out that Ben Cooper seduced her to win a bet...
and eight years since she got her revenge. Now
aboard *Alexandra's Dream* as a guest lecturer for
her cookbook, she is shocked to discover the
guest chef joining her is none other than Ben!
And when these two ex-lovers reunite, the heat
starts to climb...in and out of the kitchen!

*Available in March 2008
wherever books are sold.*

www.eHarlequin.com

HM38969

Inside ROMANCE

Stay up-to-date on all your
romance reading news!

Inside Romance is a FREE quarterly newsletter
highlighting our upcoming series releases
and promotions.

Visit
www.eHarlequin.com/InsideRomance
to sign up to receive our complimentary newsletter today!

IRNI107

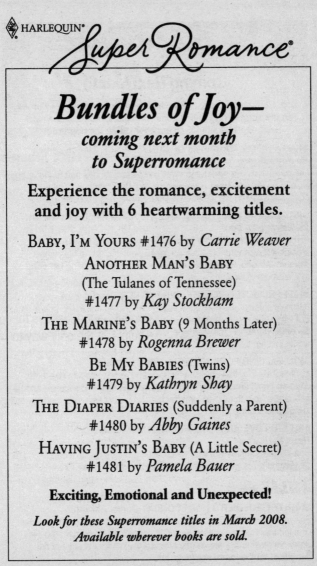

HARLEQUIN®

Super Romance®

Bundles of Joy—
coming next month to Superromance

Experience the romance, excitement and joy with 6 heartwarming titles.

BABY, I'M YOURS #1476 by *Carrie Weaver*

ANOTHER MAN'S BABY
(The Tulanes of Tennessee)
#1477 by *Kay Stockham*

THE MARINE'S BABY (9 Months Later)
#1478 by *Rogenna Brewer*

BE MY BABIES (Twins)
#1479 by *Kathryn Shay*

THE DIAPER DIARIES (Suddenly a Parent)
#1480 by *Abby Gaines*

HAVING JUSTIN'S BABY (A Little Secret)
#1481 by *Pamela Bauer*

Exciting, Emotional and Unexpected!

*Look for these Superromance titles in March 2008.
Available wherever books are sold.*

HARLEQUIN Romance

Coming Next Month

Join Harlequin Romance® in the fairy-tale mountains of Europe,
on the shimmering Italian coast, at a grand Australian estate—
and don't be late for an engagement in the boardroom!

#4009 A ROYAL MARRIAGE OF CONVENIENCE Marion Lennox
By Royal Appointment
Life doesn't always turn out the way you plan, right? As heir to the throne,
Nikolai knows duty must always come first. But country vet Rose, his
convenient wife-to-be, is not quite what Nikolai was expecting....

#4010 THE ITALIAN TYCOON AND THE NANNY Rebecca Winters
Mediterranean Dads
In the first book of this emotional duet, nanny Julie is whisked away to
a palatial Italian villa, but feels completely out of place in Massimo's
glamorous world. Her biggest challenge, though, is ignoring her attraction
to the brooding tycoon....

#4011 PROMOTED: TO WIFE AND MOTHER Jessica Hart
Perdita's efficient, no-nonsense attitude works just fine in the boardroom.
But when she meets executive Ed, and their business relationship
becomes personal, she's left wondering whether being a wife and mother
would suit her better.

#4012 FALLING FOR THE REBEL HEIR Ally Blake
It's definitely true that opposites attract, and Kendall couldn't be more
different from Hudson Bennington III. She likes safe and secure—and he's
got danger written all over him! But then he proposes a deal, and Kendall's
tempted to accept....

#4013 TO LOVE AND TO CHERISH Jennie Adams
Heart to Heart
Sometimes we think we're better off coping with hardship alone, trying to
protect the ones we love. When Jack went away he broke Tiffany's heart,
but now that his demons are behind him, he's back—and determined to
make things right.

#4014 THE SOLDIER'S HOMECOMING Donna Alward
Shannyn's beautiful daughter is a daily reminder of her true love, Jonas,
who left town to be a soldier. Now that Jonas is back, hardened by war,
Shannyn must find a way to reach his soul again for the sake of her
daughter and the family she longs for.

HRCNM0208